This book
belongs to

To my sister, Emma

FREDERICK WARNE

Published by the Penguin Group
Penguin Books Ltd, 80 Strand, London WC2R 0RL, England
Penguin Young Readers Group, 345 Hudson Street,
New York, New York 10014, U.S.A.
Penguin Books Australia Ltd, 250 Camberwell Road, Camberwell,
Victoria 3124, Australia
Canada, India, New Zealand, South Africa

1 3 5 7 9 10 8 6 4 2

ISBN: 978 0 7232 5951 0

Printed in Great Britain

Poppy's Perfect Home

By Pippa Le Quesne

Welcome to the Flower Fairies' Garden!

Where are the fairies?
Where can we find them?
We've seen the fairy-rings
They leave behind them!

Is it a secret
No one is telling?
Why, in your garden
Surely they're dwelling!

No need for journeying,
Seeking afar:
Where there are flowers,
There fairies are!

Contents

Chapter One

Terrible News
1

Chapter Two

A Welcome Visit
13

Chapter Three

A Hasty Departure
23

Chapter Four

A New Beginning
37

Chapter Five

Celebrations!
49

Chapter Six

The Homecoming
63

Chapter One
Terrible News

Poppy carefully cupped the sticky mixture first in one hand and then the other. She rolled it clockwise and then turned it over and rolled it again until she had gently shaped it into a small sphere. Then she popped it at the end of a row of balls that were lined up on a leaf in the baking sun.

"Perfect!" Poppy said, wiping her hands on the faded pink apron that she always wore when she was cooking. She'd had the apron for as long as she could remember and it had been washed so many times that it was quite thin in places. But it had been a present from her friend Tansy and the Flower Fairy firmly believed that it brought her good luck.

"Now, I definitely deserve a cup of tea," she thought out loud, feeling very pleased with the number of leaves lying on the

ground all around her. They were covered in clusters of nectar-coated poppy seeds, which were turning deliciously brittle in the heat.

It had been a hot, clear day, and Poppy had worked hard. The moon was due to be full in a few days' time and she needed to make a large batch of popcorn ready for her stall at the Fairy Fair. It was a special market that took place in a secret glade in the woods, once a month on the night of the full moon. There was music and dancing, delicious things to eat and the promise of a royal appearance from Kingcup and the Queen of the Meadow. Ever since Poppy had been old enough to attend, she hadn't missed a single one.

She had just untied her apron and was shaking some wayward seeds from the folds of her bright red dress, when she heard the sound of urgent voices.

"Poppy! Are you there?"

"Poppy— where are you?"

"I'm here," she replied, leaping in the air and beating her wings at the same time so that a moment later she was hovering just above the leafy patch. Scanning the meadow, she saw a flash of yellow in the long grass, followed immediately by another, and then she caught sight of two of the younger Flower Fairies, running in her direction.

"Buttercup, Cowslip—over here!" Poppy called cheerfully, feeling glad to have some company now that she had finished her chores. But when they turned their faces towards her, her heart missed a beat ... For instead of greeting her with their usual broad grins, the look on their faces was one of pure panic. Something was wrong. Terribly wrong.

"And you heard it from the elves?" Poppy breathed a sigh of relief. "Well, that makes me feel a lot better—it's bound to be one of their mischievous schemes to cause havoc in Flower Fairyland."

She smiled kindly at her two guests, who had cooled off after a glass of elderflower juice, but were still upset. Cowslip was shaking her head. "I know what you mean, Poppy, but these elves have been living in the hedgerow between our meadow and yours all summer, and they consider it home now. And today they were frantically packing and looked more flustered than I've ever seen them. They said they were moving straight back to the marsh—permanently."

Buttercup nodded in agreement. "It's definitely not one of their pranks. And they told us that they'd heard it from some of the fairies who live close to the farm—Ragwort and Ground Ivy—so you could always check with them." She gazed seriously at Poppy. "What are you going to do?"

"Well, if you're positive about this, then I'll call a meadow meeting right away. Now, the most helpful thing that you two can do is to go back to your side of the hedgerow and listen out for any more news. And double check that you're all safe over there, will you?" The older Flower Fairy got to her feet and, tying her apron in such a way so that it acted as a sling, she began tipping each of the leaves into it. Then she filled her two friends' pockets with some of the mouth-watering popcorn. "Thank you for coming so quickly," she said, kissing them both on their cheeks.

"Bye," Cowslip murmured. "And—we're sorry to bring you such awful news," she added.

"Don't worry," Poppy replied lightly. "There's bound to be a simple solution."

"Let us know what you decide, won't you?" Buttercup said, looking unusually serious.

"I will, of course." Poppy tried to sound as bright as possible as they exchanged goodbyes but, as she watched them flit away, she couldn't help herself from clutching her lucky apron and whispering, "Although I do hope you're wrong." Then she hurried off in the opposite direction, keen to find her meadow companions as quickly as possible.

* * *

Celandine was sobbing
into her handkerchief.
"W-w-we're d-d-
doomed!" she stuttered,
choking back a fresh wave of tears.

Stroking her friend's hand, Poppy looked
around at the group of Flower Fairies sitting
on the ground in front of her. Now that
the initial shock had passed and everyone
had stopped speaking at once—asking
her questions that she had no idea how to
answer—they were all silent, mostly staring
glumly at their laps. She was the oldest of
them and had lived in the meadow for the
longest. Celandine, Lady's-smock, Foxglove
and Fumitory always turned to her for advice
—which made her feel responsible for their
fate.

Yet, she had never been faced with such a

big problem or one that didn't seem to have a straightforward answer. She needed some time to think, and on her own. Clearing her throat, she tried to look confident.

"It's ok, leave it to me. Everyone go home and get a good night's rest and meet me back here first thing in the morning," she said reassuringly. "You don't need to be sad—I'll work something out."

"Thanks," said Foxglove, in a brave voice. "We can always count on you."

Poppy smiled and gave each one of them an encouraging pat or a hug as they left. But once they were all out of sight, the tall slender Flower Fairy crumpled back to the ground and buried her head in her arms.

"This can't be happening!" she cried. "How could anyone want to destroy our beautiful home?"

Chapter Two
A Welcome Visit

Breaking the terrible news to her friends had been the worst moment of her life. Buttercup and Cowslip had told Poppy that humans had bought the field and were planning to plough it up and replant it for farming. The fairies that lived there had always considered themselves lucky—other than the occasional group of ramblers stopping for a picnic, their peaceful existence was rarely disturbed by humans.

And now we're going to be homeless. Poppy gulped. In her right hand she held one of the strong stems of her plant. Its papery scarlet petals and intense black face towered above her.

What would happen to all of their flowers? *I've got to think of something. Everyone's depending on me*, she told herself.

Although her small chin trembled with sadness, her black wings with their jagged red edges stood proud from her back. Taking one final look and wiping away the last of her tears, she settled herself down on the hillock and prepared herself for a long night of thinking.

"Poppy?"

"Hmm?" The Flower Fairy had been deep in thought and hadn't noticed the starling landing lightly in front of her. She beamed when she recognized her friend.

Poppy could understand and talk to all

of the birds, but the starling that visited her meadow to catch grubs was her favorite by far. He was so chatty and he could never stay still for long, darting along the ground or hopping on the spot, adding a trill or a warble into his sentences as he relayed some interesting bit of gossip.

"Why the miserable face?"

"How long have you got?" Poppy sighed.

It was nearly dawn now and although she'd been thinking hard all night, she hadn't come up with any good ideas. Initially, she

had thought that if all the Flower Fairies collected together their fairy dust, they might be able to cast a spell powerful enough to protect the meadow. But it didn't take her

long to realize that it would be impossible to keep it going *forever* as their spells weren't very strong or permanent. The Flower Fairies made the magic dust from each of their individual flowers and they used it when they needed a helping hand in a tricky situation. However, this was more of a crisis and it needed a lot more than a helping hand . . .

"I've always time for you," the starling was

saying. "I'll give my feathers a preen while I'm listening."

So while he busily primped and tweaked with his pointed beak, Poppy told him all about her problem.

"Why can't you just move to the next meadow where Buttercup and Cowslip live?" the starling asked, when she'd finished.

"Well, we could," the Flower Fairy explained. "But—and I'm sure this won't happen—if we sow all our seeds there and then the farmer bought that field too and we had to move again before our flowers had grown . . . or if they didn't grow successfully. . ." Poppy blinked back the tears that were pricking her eyes. "Well, that would be it. Our flowers would become extinct."

"Oh, how dreadful! I hadn't thought of that." The starling trilled in alarm. "If there's

anything I can do, you know I'll help?"

"Yes, I know, you're a dear." Poppy smiled
in appreciation. "Now, listen, it's wonderful
to see you but I've got to come up with
something in the next couple of hours, so
it's probably best if I'm on my own."

"Absolutely, I understand,' he replied
cheerfully, smoothing down his glossy
feathers. "Oh, before I forget—I was in the
Flower Fairies' Garden yesterday and saw
our old friend Primrose. She sends her love."
And the bird dipped his beak in farewell and
took to the air.

"Thanks!" called Poppy, watching him fly away, his wings flashing purple and green in the morning sunlight. As he disappeared on the horizon, she thought how nice it must be to be able to make your home in any tree that you chose, knowing that you could fly any distance to forage for food. Or being able to travel a long way very quickly to visit friends far and wide. It took her the best part of a day to reach the Flower Fairies' Garden and the effort was exhausting.

"Oh, my," Poppy said slowly, as something that the starling had mentioned sank in. "That's it!" An idea had suddenly popped into her head, and although it might take some careful planning, it could definitely work . . .

Chapter Three
A Hasty Departure

"So . . . So, we'd have to literally abandon our plants and make our way to the garden in the hope of finding a new patch?" Foxglove looked unhappily at Poppy. "I mean—obviously I'm incredibly grateful that you've come up with a plan and it's a great idea. It's just such a shock . . ."

Foxglove was one of the most striking Flower Fairies that Poppy knew. He was clothed almost entirely in dark purple—

from the tip of his sharp-pointed shoes
right to the hood that his impish face and
angular ears poked out from. Only his jaunty
shorts weren't purple. They were gold with
burgundy spots, like the speckled insides of
his flowers. His flowers hung in bells from
a spike rising way above the Flower Fairy's
head. His plants were also one of the most
noticeable features of the meadow—the lofty
blooms visible all around the perimeter. And
Foxglove could often be found climbing
up one to get a better view or to exchange
news with the bumble bees while they were
collecting pollen.

He was such a happy, outgoing fellow
that seeing him looking so downhearted was
especially upsetting.

"I know," Poppy said gently. "It's almost
unbearable to think of. But we've so many
friends in the garden—and I've sent the

starling ahead to ask if there might be an area
large enough for us all to stay together. So
we'd still have each other."

"You're very thoughtful, Poppy." Fumitory
made this comment, but there was a general
murmur of agreement from all assembled.
"However," she went on, "I think it's best if
I stay put." Celandine opened her mouth in
surprise but shut it again when Fumitory
continued talking. "My plants have never

ever grown in the garden and as much as I would like to get to know the Flower Fairies that live there, I'm going to take my chances in Buttercup and Cowslip's meadow."

"But, it's a risk—as I explained earlier." Poppy frowned.

"I know," replied Fumitory. "But I'm more afraid that if I grow my plants in the garden then the humans will find them and, not recognizing them, will think they're weeds

and pull them out."

Celandine gasped, and seeing that she looked a bit faint, Poppy put a supportive arm around her. She glanced at the others— Lady's-smock and Foxglove appeared to be confused and she guessed that they were trying to decide which move would be for the best.

"Listen," she said. "I know what you're saying, dear Fumitory, but you've heard of

the Country Queen, haven't you?" All of
her listeners nodded to show that they had.
"Well—I'm old enough to remember when
she lived in this very meadow. Of course, she
loved it in the wild, but she knew many of the
Garden Flower Fairies and felt very at home
among them. So much so that, one day, she
decided to go and live there."

"And was she happy?" asked Lady's-
smock.

"She still is," Poppy said, with a twinkle in
her eye, "but she has a new name. I'm talking

about Primrose!"

"Primrose was the Country Queen?!" exclaimed Foxglove. "I never would have guessed. I must say that I've always been amazed at how much she knows about the meadow. But she seems, er ... tamer than us somehow, as though all she has ever known is a more ordered life."

Poppy chuckled. "There are all sorts of *different* kinds of fairies that live in the Flower Fairies' Garden. And yes, Primrose is very organized —which

is why she likes it there—but wait until you
get to know Dandelion and Sycamore!" She
turned to Fumitory. "So, what do you think?"

But before Fumitory could answer, there
was a sudden deafening roar of an engine,
and all of the Flower Fairies shot into the
nearest hedgerow, fleeing for cover.

"Gather your fairy dust and any seeds that you might have stored—and let's go!"

Poppy was trying hard not to tremble as she issued orders to her frightened friends.

Once she was sure that whatever was making the unearthly noise wasn't too close

by, she'd sent Foxglove up one of his plants to see what was going on. He'd come back, ashen-faced and shaking.

"It's—it's happening already," he'd reported, his eyes wide with fear.

"What is, Foxglove? What did you see?" Lady's-smock had asked, jumping up and down impatiently.

"A big blue tractor with the most horrific thing attached to the back of it. It was huge and metal and had lots of sharp bits on it and ... and ..."

"Take a deep breath. It's all right," Poppy had told him, although her heart was in her mouth—for she knew what he was describing was a *plough*.

"And it's ripping out the grass at the bottom of the meadow and throwing up great chunks of soil!" Foxglove gushed and then he collapsed in a heap on the ground, too upset to say anything else.

So, she'd taken a couple of deep breaths herself and then set about thinking what needed doing in the minutes that were left before they were in *real* danger.

Now, her meadow companions stood before her—each with a basket or a knapsack holding a few belongings. Poppy had put her essential possessions in her apron first thing that morning, and it hung across one shoulder, still tied as a sling. The grinding

and crashing of the machinery was now much nearer and the entire world seemed to be shaking and juddering around them.

"Obviously, we have no choice but to leave —and fast," Poppy said. "There's no time to make a proper plan now, so let's just get over to the next meadow and we'll make a decision then."

"I can't bear to even *hear* those monstrous machines," wailed Celandine, her pale green wings drooping.

"Don't worry," Poppy replied. "We're going to get far away very soon. But first things first—we need to put the hedgerow between us and the humans so that we're safe."

The other Flower Fairies nodded sadly and then, one by one, each with a forlorn backward glance at their fast-disappearing home, they reluctantly pushed their way

through the hedge.

Poppy was the final one to go. She took one last, desperate look at her vibrant flowers—swaying serenely in the breeze—and then, swallowing a painful lump in her throat, fled after her friends.

Chapter Four
A New Beginning

After an initial dash to put some distance
between themselves and the hedgerow, the
evacuees congregated at the top end of the
neighboring meadow. Now they were sitting
with Buttercup, who was doing her best
to comfort them—having made cups of tea
and offered them somewhere to sleep that
night. Only Fumitory had accepted. With
her head bowed, the little wild fairy asked

Buttercup if she might, in fact, stay with her on a semi-permanent basis while she sowed some seeds and waited for new plants to grow. She managed a half-smile when her friend warmly welcomed her to the patch, but Poppy could see how painful it was for her to watch the rest of them depart.

"Thanks for the offer, Buttercup, but we have to keep going. None of us can bear to be anywhere near the meadow while it's being destroyed." Poppy swallowed hard. Despite all that had happened and the fact that she was surviving on only an hour's sleep, she managed to fight back the tears. She had to stay strong for the other Flower Fairies. They still had a long way to go and someone had to take command.

"Listen," Buttercup said. "The humans are probably going to be driving back and forth all day on the lane and the quickest way to the

Flower Fairies' Garden is to cross it. Now,
I know that they're busy with this horrible
ploughing business," she said this last bit in
a respectfully hushed voice, "but humans are
never too busy to ignore the sight of fairies
… It's just too risky—"

"I know, Buttercup, and we'll do
everything we can to make sure they don't
spot us," Poppy
interrupted, only
too aware that they
would be putting
Flower Fairyland
in peril if any of the

farm laborers caught sight of them.

"Wait." Buttercup held up a hand. "I was going to say, let me sprinkle some fairy dust on you all just as you leave—and with the right spell it'll act as an invisible mantle and get you safely across. You'll have to be quick as it'll be spread quite thinly among you—but it should work."

Poppy gratefully agreed on behalf of the others and she could see the look of relief on Lady's-smock's face. Like her flowers, Lady's-smock was pale and petite and the journey was going to be gruelling enough for her without the extra element of danger.

"OK, then, huddle close—and here, Fumitory, you take a handful too," Buttercup instructed, holding out the chestnut leaf she'd just unfolded.

"Thank you, my dears—we shall be perfectly safe because of you," Poppy said, smiling bravely at Buttercup and then Fumitory, whose eyes were brimming with unshed tears. "And we'll come back and visit you soon. Now—on the count of three—" She checked to see that Lady's-smock, Celandine and Foxglove were ready to take flight. "One . . . two . . . three!"

On her command, the two Flower Fairies threw the miniscule particles of fairy dust over them and, simultaneously, the departing friends opened their wings and took to the air.

"Fairy dust, fairy dust, hide them from view, help them fly quickly and safely too," called Buttercup.

And, as the cloud of fine powder began to twinkle and sparkle, the four fairies gradually vanished from sight, until the only clue to their whereabouts was a shimmering haze that moved swiftly over the top of the hedgerow and disappeared into the lane beyond . . .

Poppy sat, hugging her knees, staring up at the stars. *They're still the same*, she thought to herself, *so not everything has changed.*

Although she was more exhausted than she could ever remember, her head was buzzing with the events of what had felt like the longest day of her life.

Despite the sudden rattling of a tractor, which had given them all a tremendous

fright, the four Flower Fairies had kept their
course and made it safely across the lane
before the fairy dust had worn off. Then they
had flown as far as their wings could take

them before landing in the middle of the vast
expanse of marsh. There, the travellers had
been surprised and delighted to be met by
Mallow, who had heard whisperings on the
breeze that they were coming. She'd given
each of them one of her special fairy cheeses,
which filled their hungry stomachs and

cheered them up enormously.

When it was time to start moving again, their wings were still aching too much to fly any further, so they set off on foot, determined to complete their journey before the sun set. And Cotton-Grass and Rush-Grass—Mallow's friends, who were guides—had offered to show them the quickest route across the marsh to the lane on the other side.

But when Poppy and her jaded companions bade them farewell and watched them fly off into the dusk, every one of them agreed that although it was only a short distance to go now, they were all too impossibly tired to make it.

Poppy had

just begun to seek out a suitable section of bush for them to crawl under for the night, when a rapid series of chirrups alerted her to the arrival of two starlings. And there was her dear friend, and his mate, ready to take them to the special patch that they had found—a place that the kind Garden Fairies said they could call their own!

We've been so fortunate today, Poppy thought, glancing at Foxglove, Celandine and Lady's-smock, who were sleeping peacefully, curled up on the ground around her.

It was getting dark when the two birds alighted in the bottom corner of the garden and most of the Flower Fairies were in bed, but there was Rose to greet them—with cups of chamomile tea and warm moss blankets and promises of a proper welcome the next morning.

"So this is our new . . ." Poppy couldn't

bring herself to even whisper the word. She was incredibly grateful that they had made it safely to the garden and she'd been bowled over by all the help they'd had on the way. And she knew that, given time, they'd all be very happy there, but just at that moment it was impossible to think of anywhere but the meadow as home.

Celandine sighed and turned over in her sleep and Poppy smiled to see her peaceful little face. "But we're still all together," she said softly, making herself comfortable and laying down her head for the night, "and that's the most important thing."

Chapter Five
Celebrations!

"Wake up, Poppy! Wake up!"

Poppy groaned and opened one eye. It was Foxglove, looking fit to burst about something.

"What time is it?" The sleepy Flower Fairy sat up and stretched. It felt *very* early.

"Never mind that," replied her friend impatiently. "You've got to come and see this!" And without further ado, Foxglove turned on his heel and disappeared around the back of the rose bushes.

Three whole seasons had passed since Poppy and the others had come to live in the garden. Rose had dedicated a corner of her secret rose garden to them and they had set about making a new home and sowing their seeds. They had dug themselves an allotment and lovingly fed and watered the soil to give their plants the best possible chance to flourish. And then they had waited.

Then, one bright spring morning, the four meadow friends were rewarded for their hard work. One of Celandine's tender green shoots pushed its way through the earth and gradually unfurled. Soon, others came to join it and the allotment was dotted with yellow stars, and it was not long before Lady's-smock's dainty mauve flowers were all around the patch too. And since the larks had hailed the start of summer, Foxglove and Poppy had anxiously awaited their turn.

"Could this be it?" Poppy said to herself, springing to her feet and hurrying over the dewy grass.

As she rounded the thorny bush, now adorned with heavenly scented blooms, she gasped. For there, in front of her, were not only a dozen stunning foxgloves— standing tall and strong—but several clumps of her own glorious poppies, bobbing around on their bendy stems with their waxy red petals and sooty faces.

"We've done it!" she yelled, flinging her arms around Foxglove, who was beaming from ear to ear. "We've done it!"

"Mmmm, mmm," mumbled Candytuft, her mouth so full of popcorn that Poppy couldn't make out what she was saying.

"I may have lost my touch," said Poppy nervously. "I mean it's practically been a year since I last made any popcorn." She looked shyly down at her old pink apron, which until now had remained folded up, unused

for just as long.

Since their flight to the garden, Poppy hadn't attended the Fairy Fair. Other than one trip back to the meadow—which had been nothing more than neatly ploughed earth and such a distressing sight that she'd resolved not to return—she hadn't really ventured into the wild. She'd also stopped going to the moonlit market because she hadn't wanted to run her popcorn stall for fear of using up her scant supply of poppy seeds in case the planted ones didn't flower. But now that *all* the meadow flowers had successfully bloomed, the four friends had decided to throw a party to celebrate and also to thank the Garden Flower Fairies for their wonderful hospitality. And, of course, a party wouldn't be complete without special treats!

"It's absolutely delicious!" announced Candytuft, swallowing the last mouthful.

"You haven't lost your touch at all." She licked her lips in appreciation. "Gosh—I really have missed your popcorn."

Poppy grinned. Candytuft was renowned for the adventurous sweet delicacies that she created, so her approval was very important.

"Excellent," Poppy said. "And thanks for your help. Right I've got work to do—we'll see you this evening just after sunset. Don't be late!"

"I won't!" promised Candytuft, skipping round the rose bush and back into the main garden.

* * *

"Foxglove, Foxglove,
What see you now?
The soft summer moonlight
On bracken, grass, and bough;
And all the fairies dancing
As only they know how."

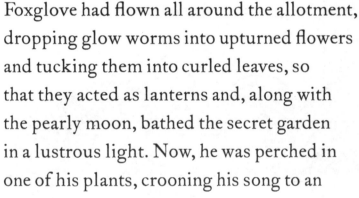

Foxglove had flown all around the allotment, dropping glow worms into upturned flowers and tucking them into curled leaves, so that they acted as lanterns and, along with the pearly moon, bathed the secret garden in a lustrous light. Now, he was perched in one of his plants, crooning his song to an

appreciative audience of Flower Fairies, who laughed and clapped at the words.

Overflowing bowls of freshly toasted popcorn nestled in the grass, and there were other goodies such as walnut and date cake, crystallized honeycomb, and rosewater punch. All the guests had arrived in their most gorgeous outfits and the scene was

spectacular. The party had only just started but the starlings were on hand to warble out tunes to accompany the dancing, and everyone appeared to be in a celebratory mood.

"You've all settled in so well," said Primrose, an arm around her friend's shoulder, "that it's hard to remember a time when you didn't live here."

Poppy nodded appreciatively. They were sitting together on a mushroom stool, soaking up the atmosphere and chatting. It was true—Foxglove had become popular for his entertaining company and when he wasn't busy in the allotment he could be found tearing through the garden with the likes of Dandelion, Sycamore and Cornflower. And Celandine and Lady's-smock had become best friends with quiet Jasmine and thoughtful Rose. She too had had a happy time—she'd enjoyed seeing more of Tansy and Primrose and she'd got to know Sweet Pea, who often dropped by with her sister and a gaggle of the baby fairies. The garden was a fantastic place to live—there was always something fun going on. But somehow, Poppy's heart still ached for meadow life. She longed to hear the crickets chirping on a warm evening, or to witness the newborn field mice first opening their eyes, or to drink the dew that had gathered overnight on the enormous leaves. She missed it all.

Primrose was giving her a knowing look. "You should go back, you know."

Poppy was jolted from her thoughts.

"I've seen that faraway look of yours." Her friend laughed. "And now you've got some more seeds, there's no real excuse."

Poppy looked at her enquiringly.

"If the feeling's there, it'll never go away. And one day, you'll wake up and think you've got too many roots here and that it's too late." Primrose slid off the mushroom and smiled. "I'm going to get a another drink" she said,

waving her cup. "Think about it!"

The nimble Flower Fairy disappeared into the throng and Poppy found herself alone. She gazed up at the stars and sighed.

Is Primrose right? she wondered. *Is it really time to go back to the wild?*

Chapter Six
The Homecoming

"Right. All set?"

Poppy nodded at Foxglove. Then she grinned at Tansy, who stood at the front of the crowd of Flower Fairies that had gathered to see her off, and patted her apron sling. "The last time I wore this, it brought us all here safely. And we may have lost the meadow that day but we gained a lot of very dear friends." She looked sheepishly round at them all. "So, I'm hoping that my lucky apron will bring me the same good fortune today and find me a new home."

"What's your plan?" Celandine said quietly, slipping her small hand into Poppy's.

"I'm going back to Buttercup and Cowslip's field to see where Fumitory has settled."

"We all wish you the best of luck," Primrose interjected. "And remember— there'll always be a home for you here."

"That's right," Rose added. "I'll make sure your poppies continue to thrive."

"Yes, we'll take care of them." Lady's-smock looked up at Poppy. "But you'll come back and visit, won't you?"

"Of course I will!" exclaimed the older Flower Fairy. "I'd miss you all too much if I didn't." Then, taking one last glance round the secret garden, which she'd grown immensely fond of, she clambered on to the back of the starling, who was waiting to carry

her off. "Farewell! I'll be back at the Fairy
Fair soon, if all goes well. Enjoy the rest of
the party!"

Wrapping her arms around the bird's
neck, she whispered to him that she was
ready to go. And as her stomach began to
churn with anticipation, the starling flapped
his strong wings and soon they were soaring
high above the garden.

Poppy opened her eyes.

The sun was higher in
the sky than when she
usually woke and its
warmth had stirred
her from her sleep.
She got up and
stretched, taking
huge lungfuls of
country air. It felt *so*

good to be back and she couldn't remember the last time she had slept so well.

Fumitory had been just about to turn in for the night when the starling had dropped Poppy off, but she'd been thrilled to see her old friend and they'd sat up talking until their eyelids were heavy and neither of them could stay awake any longer.

"Good morning!" It was Fumitory. "I've been gathering wild strawberries."

"Oooh, lovely, I'm starved," said Poppy, thinking that all her senses seemed more acute in the wild and that she was hungrier than usual.

"Well, bring a couple with you—there's something I've been

67

dying to show you." replied Fumitory,
producing a handkerchief from her pocket.
"But it's a surprise, so I'm going to blindfold
you."

"Blindfold me?!" Poppy giggled, then
taking a huge bite of a sweet berry, stood still

obediently while her friend secured the petal strip over her eyes.

"Here—take my hand. We're going to fly but I'll guide you," Fumitory instructed.

So, hand in hand, flapping their gossamer wings, the two Flower Fairies took off. It was an odd sensation for Poppy—flying, but not knowing where she was heading—however she trusted her friend completely and a thrill of excitement went through her.

They hadn't covered a very large distance when Fumitory directed them back down to the ground and let go of Poppy's hand.

"Are you ready?" She began untying the handkerchief. "OK—here goes . . . Surprise!"

It took a moment for Poppy's eyes to adjust to the light but when they did, they were met by a remarkable sight. "Oh my goodness!" she said, quite simply. "But where are we?"

For they had landed at the top end of a field that was furrowed and obviously farmland. However, atop the mounds of soil, swathes of wild flowers were growing. There were clusters of Fumitory's plants—with their feathery blue-green foliage and tiny pink flowers which gave the impression of smoke billowing across the earth. And . . . Poppy couldn't believe her eyes—there were clumps of *her* resplendent scarlet flowers scattered *all over* the meadow.

"It's *our* meadow, Poppy. I don't know how it's happened, but it really is." Fumitory held out a steadying hand to her friend. "The birds tell me they've seen it happen before— varieties of flowers that are so stubborn that they'll grow anywhere—no matter what!"

"It's incredible," breathed Poppy.

"I know," replied Fumitory. "I only discovered this a few days ago—despite living so close, I've been avoiding coming here." Her face was wet with tears. "It's so good to have you back, Poppy. I didn't want to send for you as I thought you might be happy in the garden and I didn't want to make it difficult for you, but—"

"I was happy," Poppy interrupted. "But I could never *ever* be happier than here in our meadow. And just like our flowers—I'm never going to leave it."

She turned to Fumitory and squeezed her hand in appreciation. Then, feeling as though her heart would burst for joy, she whooped and set off down the meadow, shouting at the top of her voice, "We're home! We're really home!"

Visit our Flower Fairies website at:

www.flowerfairies.com

There are lots of fun Flower Fairy games and activities for you to play, plus you can find out more about all your favorite fairy friends!

Log onto the
Flower Fairies
Friendship Ring

Visit the Flower Fairies website to sign up for the new Flower Fairies Friendship Ring!

★ No membership fee
★ News and updates
★ Every new friend receives a special gift!
(while supplies last)

CÉDRIC

Dîner-surprise

RETROUVEZ **CÉDRIC**

DANS LA BIBLIOTHÈQUE ROSE

Moi, j'aime l'école

Mon papa est astronaute

La fête de l'école

Roulez, jeunesse !

La photo

J'aime pas les vacances

Maladie d'amour

Tout est dans la tête

Des rollers à tout prix

Votez pour moi !

Nos amies les bêtes

Pépé boude

Dîner-surprise

CÉDRIC

CAUVIN - Laudec

Dîner-surprise

Adaptation : Claude Carré

HACHETTE

1

Dîner-surprise

Mon pépé, il est vraiment impossible. Il est coléreux, râleur et têtu. Mais surtout, il ne plaisante pas avec la nourriture. Jamais. Quand ça ne lui plaît pas, il le dit. Le problème, c'est que papa, lui, ne supporte pas qu'on critique la cuisine de maman. Alors évidemment, un jour, il y a eu un petit couac. Et quand je dis un petit…

On avait plutôt bien mangé, ce soir-là, mais à la fin du repas on s'est rendu compte que l'assiette de pépé était toujours pleine. Il semblait faire la tête, avec les bras croisés et les sourcils froncés. Maman, bien sûr, s'est tout de suite inquiétée. À l'âge de pépé, quand on n'a pas faim, ça cache souvent quelque chose de plus grave.

— Qu'est-ce qui se passe, papa ? Tu n'as rien mangé…

Très vite, on a été rassurés. Pépé allait parfaitement bien. Il était juste contrarié, et il tenait à le faire savoir :

— J'aime pas le potiron, a-t-il râlé,
la viande n'était pas assez cuite, et
j'ai horreur du fenouil !

Il avait dit ça sur un ton bougon,
et rien n'énervait plus papa que ces
caprices d'enfant gâté. Il a tout de
suite attaqué, pendant que je m'é-
loignais discrètement :

— Dites donc, vous ! Si vous n'êtes
pas content, vous n'avez qu'à la
faire, la cuisine !

Pépé a aussitôt répliqué, en se
penchant par-dessus la table :

— Parce que vous ne m'en croyez
pas capable ?

Papa s'est levé de son siège et s'est penché, lui aussi, par-dessus la table. Leurs deux nez étaient maintenant appuyés l'un contre l'autre.

— Capable ? Ah ah ah ! Vous ne seriez même pas fichu de cuire un œuf au plat !

— Ça, c'est trop fort ! s'est étranglé pépé.

— Robert ! a crié maman.

Mais le mal était fait. Pépé a serré les mâchoires, sans rien dire. Puis il s'est levé, a jeté sa serviette sur la nappe d'un geste sec et a quitté la table.

— Papa, où vas-tu ?

Avant de franchir la porte, pépé

s'est retourné pour répondre :

— Au lit ! J'ai besoin de réfléchir ! Demain soir, c'est moi qui m'occupe du dîner !

Maman a ouvert de grands yeux.

— Mais enfin papa, c'est ridicule !

— C'est ce qu'on va voir ! a crié pépé avant de monter dans sa chambre.

Le lendemain matin, quand il est descendu pour le petit déjeuner, j'étais déjà installé dans le canapé du salon, avec une bonne B.D. Je l'ai salué :

— Bonjour, pépé ! Alors, c'est vrai ?

Tu vas faire à manger, ce soir ? Ça tient toujours ?

— Ben, a-t-il commencé…

Mais papa, qui rentrait au même moment, lui a coupé la parole :

— Mais oui ! a-t-il ricané ; et comme ce sera immangeable, on ira au restaurant ! ET IL LA MANGERA TOUT SEUL, SA TAMBOUILLE !

Pépé a porté la main à son cœur, comme s'il avait reçu un coup d'épée. Il semblait vraiment vexé.

— MA QUOI ?

— VOTRE TAMBOUILLE !!!

En levant les yeux vers pépé, je lui ai timidement demandé :

— Tu veux que je vienne avec toi faire des courses ?

Il s'est dirigé vers l'entrée et a enfilé son manteau d'un geste grandiose, comme s'il se drapait dans sa dignité.

— Non, merci ! Je préfère me débrouiller tout seul ! C'est une

question d'honneur entre ton père et moi !

Avant qu'il sorte, papa a remarqué les yeux furibonds de maman ; alors, il a maladroitement essayé de rattraper le coup, d'une voix un peu adoucie :

— Dites, beau-père... Vous... Vous ne voulez pas un peu d'argent, pour...

C'était un peu tard. Pépé a posé

sa main sur la poignée de la porte d'entrée, a redressé la tête et a déclaré, les yeux mi-clos :

— Ma pension n'a que la peau sur les os, mais tant qu'elle aura un souffle de vie, elle ne demandera rien à personne !

Et il est sorti en claquant violemment la porte derrière lui. On a été impressionnés. Seulement voilà : pépé, ça fait au moins dix ans qu'il n'avait pas fait les courses ! Il allait trouver les prix rudement changés ! Je ne pouvais pas le laisser comme ça, il avait besoin de mon aide ! Alors j'ai pris une décision très grave.

Je suis monté quatre à quatre jusqu'à ma chambre et je suis allé
cherché ma tirelire sur mon bureau.
Quand je l'ai secouée, elle a fait un
bruit de pas grand-chose. Mais tant
pis, même pas grand-chose, ça lui
serait sans doute utile à pépé ! Et je
l'ai fracassée au sol.

Mes quelques pièces à la main, je
suis sorti à mon tour, ventre à terre,

sans prendre le temps de dire à maman où j'allais. Et j'ai couru, couru jusqu'au centre-ville. Je n'ai pas tardé à repérer pépé. Il venait tout juste de tourner le coin de la rue commerçante. J'ai crié :

— Pépé, pépé !

Il s'est retourné et m'a regardé arriver, tout surpris.

— Qu'est-ce que tu viens faire là ?

J'ai freiné comme j'ai pu et je me suis raccroché à lui pour ne pas perdre l'équilibre. Tout essouflé, j'ai bredouillé d'un ton gêné :

— C'est que... Hum... J'ai pensé... Tu sais, pour préparer un bon dîner, il faut beaucoup de sous, alors…

J'ai sorti les pièces de ma poche, quatre euros au total, et je les lui ai tendues :

— Tiens !

Il s'est penché vers moi, l'air sincèrement ému :

— Ça, c'est drôlement gentil, gamin ! Mais tu sais, je vais bien arriver à me débrouiller tout seul…

Il a refermé mes doigts autour des pièces, pour que je les remette dans ma poche, et il a continué son chemin.

Tout seul, ce n'était quand même pas très prudent. Alors j'ai préféré l'accompagner quand même. Mais sans qu'il s'en rende compte, en restant à bonne distance derrière lui et en me cachant. Il a commencé par

entrer dans la boucherie. Avant
que la porte se referme, j'ai pu
entendre le début de la conversation :

— Bonjour, monsieur. Qu'est-ce
que je vous sers ?

— Un bon rosbif, pour quatre
personnes, s'il vous plaît !

Après, je n'ai plus rien entendu.
Mais par la vitrine, je les ai vus dis-
cuter, le boucher et lui. Et puis j'ai
vu pépé devenir tout rouge, rouge

comme le rosbif qu'il n'a pas acheté !
Il s'est dirigé vers la sortie, et j'ai
juste eu le temps de me plaquer le
dos contre un mur.

Quand il ouvert la porte, toute la
rue a pu entendre :

— Quinze euros pour un rosbif !
À ce prix-là, vous pouvez le garder,
votre morceau de barbaque !

M. Blondiot, le boucher, n'avait
pas l'habitude de se laisser marcher
sur les pieds. À son tour, il s'est mis
à crier :

— Si c'est trop cher pour votre
porte-monnaie, z'avez qu'à acheter
une livre de rognons à la place !

— Ah dites donc, restez poli, vous !
a fait pépé en s'éloignant.

J'ai hésité et puis finalement je
suis sorti de ma cachette. En trotti-
nant, j'ai rejoint mon pépé. Il était
drôlement énervé, j'ai eu du mal à
le rattraper. Quand il m'a aperçu, il
m'a dit :

— T'es encore là, toi ? Non mais t'as vu ? Quel escroc, ce boucher !

— Je t'avais prévenu, pépé : c'est devenu cher, la viande !

Hélas, il n'y avait pas que la viande ! Un peu plus loin, on est passés devant un étal de fruits et légumes, et pépé s'est arrêté. Il a commencé à tâter quelque belles salades ; quand il en a choisi une, il a demandé à la marchande combien il lui devait.

— Trois euros, monsieur !

Là, j'ai cru que les yeux de pépé allaient lui sortir de la tête.

— TROIS EUROS, UNE LAITUE ! ÇA VA PAS, LA TÊTE !

J'ai dû intervenir et l'emmener un peu plus loin.

— Calme-toi, pépé... Allez, viens !

— Non mais je rêve !

Il m'a suivi, mais il ne semblait toujours pas comprendre. Et ça ne s'est pas arrangé lorsqu'on est arrivés devant le tournebroche installé à l'extérieur de la rôtisserie. De superbes poulets s'y doraient la peau du dos et ça sentait drôlement bon. Mais quand il a entendu le prix que lui en demandait le charcutier, pépé a explosé.

— HEIN !!! Vous les avez nourris au caviar, ou quoi ? À ce prix-là, vous savez où vous pouvez vous les mettre, vos poulets ?

— Pépé !

J'ai encore une fois réussi à l'entraîner hors de portée du vendeur, qui voulait lui donner un coup de dindon sur la tête. Le problème de mon pépé, c'est qu'il est très très orgueilleux. Il ne s'avoue jamais vaincu. Jamais. Pour ce fichu repas, il refusait d'abandonner, même si ce n'était pas dans ses moyens. Et il ne voulait toujours pas de mes sous !

Il est allé s'asseoir tout seul un peu plus loin sur un banc, en bordure du parc. Il s'était calmé, mais du coup, il ne disait plus rien. Il avait les yeux éteints, et il regardait fixement le sol devant lui, comme

hypnotisé. Puis je suis revenu vers lui et j'ai essayé de faire la conversation, pour lui donner des idées :

— Dis, je pourrais t'aider à faire des crêpes ? Ça a l'air facile, quand maman en fait !

Il n'a rien dit, n'a pas bougé d'un poil. Je pense qu'à ce moment-là, même s'il avait reçu une crotte de pigeon sur le nez, il n'aurait pas bronché. Il a fallu que je trouve autre chose :

— Ou bien des œufs durs. Ça doit pas être compliqué, des œufs durs, et pas cher, en plus. On commence par... Enfin, d'abord, il faut... Bon, et puis on n'a qu'à trouver la recette, et le tour est joué !

Soudain, il s'est dressé d'un bond, des étincelles dans le regard, les cils au garde-à-vous.

— J'ai trouvé ! s'est-il exclamé.

J'ai levé les yeux vers lui, interloqué.

— Tu as trouvé quoi, pépé ?

Mais déjà il était reparti, d'un bon pas. Il m'a lancé un clin d'œil, par-dessus son épaule :

— Hé hé, tu le verras bien ce soir, au dîner !

J'ai compris qu'il venait d'avoir l'idée d'une surprise, et je dois dire qu'on n'a pas été déçus. Quand papa est revenu du travail, en fin d'après-midi, il était d'excellente humeur.

— Bonsoir tout le monde ! a-t-il fait en entrant dans le salon. J'ai une faim de loup, moi ! Qu'est-ce qu'il nous a préparé, ce vieux filou ?

Du doigt, maman lui a indiqué la porte de cuisine.

— On n'en sait toujours rien ! Regarde !

Papa s'est gaiement approché de la porte, pour mieux lire le papier qui y avait été scotché.

— « Entrée interdite » a-t-il lu... Ouh là, ça devient sérieux !

Maman était moyennement confiante. Le front un peu plissé, elle a raconté :

— Tout à l'heure, il m'a demandé de lui expliquer le fonctionnement du four, et il a fait de la place devant

la fenêtre. Depuis, il s'est enfermé à l'intérieur. Faut pas le déranger, il a dit !

Papa a considéré qu'il avait quand même le droit de savoir ce qui se passait chez lui ; il a frappé un petit coup, juste pour voir. Une tornade a soufflé de l'autre côté, faisant trembler la porte et sursauter papa :

— ENTRÉE INTERDITE ! SAVEZ PAS LIRE ?

Vexé, papa est reparti à la charge, tout décoiffé, et sur le même ton :

— ALORS, QUAND EST-CE QU'ON MANGE ?

— SEPT HEURES TAPANTES ! a répondu la tornade, de l'intérieur de la cuisine.

J'ai jeté un coup d'œil à la pendule. C'était pour bientôt ! J'avais non seulement faim, mais j'étais surtout piqué par la curiosité : quelle sorte de surprise pépé avait-il donc préparée ? Même moi, il n'avait rien voulu me dire. J'ai aidé maman à mettre le couvert et on s'est installés à table. Du coin de l'œil, je surveillais la grande aiguille de la pendule qui chatouillait le 12 sur le cadran de l'horloge.

— Je me demande si pépé…

Papa ne m'a pas laissé terminer ma phrase :

— Cesse de t'inquiéter pour ce vieux filou ! Il a voulu cuisiner, qu'il se débrouille !

Au même instant, et tandis que la pendule sonnait les sept coups, la porte de la cuisine s'est ouverte.

Pépé est apparu dans l'encadrement, droit comme un i, avec sa
chemise bien repassée, et un tor-
chon sur le bras. Il tenait un long
plat ovale, qu'il est venu déposer
délicatement au milieu de la nappe,
devant nous.

Alors qu'on ouvrait de grands
yeux devant son service impeccable,

il a annoncé, d'une voix de maître d'hôtel, élégante et distinguée :

— Marinade de saumon fumé à l'aneth et au radis noir !

On en est restés muets. Ça avait l'air si appétissant qu'on n'allait peut-être même pas oser l'entamer, la marinade de saumon ! De l'autre main, il tenait une bouteille de vin blanc, tout juste sortie de son seau à glace. Il a commencé à servir maman, avant de remplir le verre de papa.

— Pinot blanc, Domaine Palinsac 1989 !

Puis, en se tournant vers moi, il a plaisanté :

— Et eau minérale 2005 pour toi, gamin !

Une fois nos verres remplis, il est reparti dans la cuisine pour s'occuper de la suite. On est restés silencieux un moment, papa, maman et moi, tout en couvant des yeux le poisson qui marinait. Finalement maman nous a servis. Alors on s'est jetés sur nos assiettes, comme si on n'avait pas mangé depuis une semaine. La bouche pleine, j'ai réussi à dire :

— Hummm !... ch'est rudement bon !

— Il se débrouille plus que bien, ton pépé, a approuvé maman.

— Là, a ajouté papa qui savourait son saumon, je dois dire qu'il remonte dans mon estime. C'est l'un de mes plats préférés !

Et on n'en était qu'à l'entrée ! Si

ça continuait, à la fin du repas, ils allaient tomber dans les bras l'un de l'autre ! Même l'eau n'avait pas le même goût que d'habitude. On a mis une part de côté pour le chef cuistot, et on a soigneusement saucé nos assiettes, avec de larges tranches de pain. Comme s'il avait deviné qu'on avait terminé, pépé est revenu, avec la suite du menu. Il s'est approché de la table et s'est penché en avant pour nous présenter le plat de résistance :

— Noisette de chevreuil à la Normande !

C'était encore mieux qu'au restaurant ; ça sentait si bon et c'était si bien présenté que je me suis remis à saliver. Pépé avait même pensé au vin rouge pour accompagner la viande ; il a fait tourner la bouteille dans sa main, pour qu'on en voie bien l'étiquette:

— Château Saint-Valéry 1986.

J'ai demandé en souriant :

— Pépé, il reste de l'eau minérale 2005 pour moi ?

— Mais bien sûr, gamin !

Et il m'a servi comme si j'étais le

jeune prince du royaume voisin.
Quand il est reparti, maman a commencé à s'interroger :

— Mais enfin… Comment a-t-il pu ?

Papa se régalait tellement qu'il ne
se posait même plus de questions.

— Je n'en sais rien, mais c'est
réussi ! Tout à fait délicieux !

Il s'en fallait de peu pour que
maman commence à se sentir vexée.

D'habitude, papa ne fait jamais tant
de « slurps ! » et de « hum » quand il
dîne avec nous. Après avoir attaqué
une noisette de chevreuil, j'ai donné
mon avis :

— Ah oui, alors ! Fantastiquement
délicieux !

Maman m'a lancé un regard noir et fait comme si elle boudait son plat, en laissant sur le bord de son assiette quelques pieds de champignons « pas très cuits », selon elle. Bref, on a mangé comme des ogres, papa et moi ; à la fin, on avait de la sauce jusque sur le bout du nez. Il ne nous restait plus grand-place pour le dessert, mais il n'était pas question de le rater. On allait en trouver, de la place, même si on devait se rendre malade !

Et justement, pépé sortait de la cuisine avec, sur un plateau, quatre gros ramequins débordant de crème glacée. À côté des ramequins, il y

avait une bouteille de jus de fruits. Tout en disposant sur la table les couverts à dessert, il a annoncé :

— Mandarine glacée à la mousse de chocolat blanc ! J'apporte les cafés dans un instant. Et jus de mandarines pour toi, gamin !

Papa a desserré un peu sa cravate. Il était un peu gai, grâce au vin, et il a tenu à féliciter pépé :

— C'est succulent, beau-papa ! Vous avez décidément des talents cachés !

Modestement, pépé a répondu :

— Je suis content que ça vous ait plu...

— Mais tous ces produits de première qualité, a continué papa, ça a
dû vous coûter les yeux de la tête !
Je... je tiens à participer aux frais.

— Ah, bon, mais c'est que…

Papa a insisté :

— Si si, c'est tout à fait normal…

Il avait déjà sorti son portefeuille
et comptait des billets. Et là, on a
commencé à voir que pépé devenait
un peu gêné. Il s'est gratté la tête,
s'est entortillé la moustache et a
toussoté :

— Hum hum… C'est que…

— Non, non, s'il vous plaît, ne
discutez pas… Combien voulez-vous ?

Alors, pépé a fait signe à papa de
le suivre jusque dans la cuisine.

— En fait, je ne sais pas. Venez
avec moi.

Un peu surpris, papa s'est levé et
lui a emboîté le pas. Maman et moi,
on s'est regardés un moment, sans
trop comprendre, puis on s'est levés

aussi. On les a suivis, pour ne rien rater de la suite. La fenêtre de la cuisine était grande ouverte et dans l'encadrement, dehors, il y avait un homme en blouse blanche. On ne voyait que son buste, il croisait les bras en souriant.

— Voilà ! a dit pépé : ce charmant jeune homme va vous dire combien ça fait !

Le type a hoché la tête et a sorti de sa poche une longue feuille de papier qui ressemblait à une facture. Il a fait :

— Messieurs dames, bonjour ! Nous acceptons les chèques, le liquide et les cartes de crédit.

On a vu papa sursauter. Il a été secoué par un hoquet et ce n'était pas à cause de sa digestion. Il a pointé son doigt vers le livreur qui était dans son jardin et a dit, d'une voix tremblante :

— Mais qu'est-ce que…

Pépé a pris la facture des mains du jeune homme qui souriait toujours et l'a tendue à papa, en regardant ailleurs. En lisant le chiffre inscrit tout en bas de la colonne de chiffres, papa a été pris d'un malaise. Il a dû s'appuyer contre le montant du buffet pour ne pas finir par terre. Il a sans doute voulu dire quelque chose d'important, mais on n'a entendu que :

— RHAAAAA !!!

Comme il semblait incapable d'a-
jouter autre chose, on est allés voir
de plus près ce qui se passait. Une
fois à la fenêtre, on a tout compris,
maman et moi. Il y avait une
camionnette de livraison, garée
juste devant chez nous, et des
employés finissaient de rapporter
tout leur matériel à l'intérieur. Ils
avaient tout livré par la fenêtre, et

pépé avait juste joué le rôle du maître d'hôtel. Ils portaient tous la même tenue blanche et, sur la camionnette, était inscrit le nom d'un charcutier-traiteur célèbre. Un traiteur connu dans tout le pays comme étant le traiteur des vedettes et des têtes couronnées.

— Tu as fait appel à un traiteur ! s'est écriée maman, qui donnait des petites gifles à papa pour essayer de le ranimer.

— Et alors ? a répondu pépé. Vous vouliez que je m'occupe du repas, c'est bien ce qu'on avait décidé, oui ou non ?

Papa a fini par se remettre. Il a sorti son chéquier et l'a rempli à grands coups de stylo rageurs. En le tendant au jeune homme planté devant la fenêtre, il a hurlé :

— TENEZ !

Le livreur a bien vérifié la somme, a plié soigneusement le chèque et

sans cesser de sourire, nous a lancé :

— Au revoir, messieurs dames. Merci de votre accueil. N'hésitez pas à faire appel à nous pour une prochaine occasion !

Pendant qu'il s'éloignait et rejoignait sa camionnette, papa l'a accompagné à sa façon :

— C'EST ÇA OUI ! SÛREMENT ! COMPTEZ SUR NOUS, ESCROCS !

Et il s'est retourné vers pépé d'un geste brusque avec des éclairs assassins dans les yeux ; il a même avancé les mains vers lui :

— AAAAAAH !!! RETENEZ-MOI OU JE L'ÉTRANGLE !

Mais pépé lui a tenu tête, les sourcils en bataille et commençant à retrousser ses manches.

— Oh dites, eh ! Ne faites pas cette tête-là, vous ! Vous ne vouliez pas que je participe aux frais !

Plus ils s'énervaient les uns et les autres et plus j'avais envie de rire. Mais il fallait bien que je me retienne pour que papa ne s'énerve pas davantage ! Même maman s'en est mêlée :

— C'est vrai, Robert ! C'est toi qui a insisté pour payer !

— C'EST ÇA ! DÉFENDS-LE, TOI ! IL N'ÉTAIT PAS OBLIGÉ DE FAIRE APPEL AU TRAITEUR LE PLUS CHER DU PAYS, NON PLUS !!!

— Ah écoutez, hein ! s'est défendu pépé : j'ai pris le premier sur la liste, dans l'annuaire téléphonique !

Au même instant, la sonnerie de la porte d'entrée a retenti et je suis allé ouvrir. C'était Christian. Il avait l'air tout étonné ; il a tout de suite dit :

— Ben dis donc ! Qu'est-ce qui se passe chez toi ? On entend hurler jusqu'au bout de la rue !

Je lui ai glissé :

— Bouge pas, je reviens !

Je suis reparti dans la cuisine en dérapant dans les virages. Ça ne s'était pas beaucoup calmé. Papa hurlait toujours :

— D'ACCORD, J'AI INSISTÉ ! MAIS JE NE PENSAIS PAS QUE MON SALAIRE DU MOIS ALLAIT Y PASSER !

J'ai pris maman à part :

— M'man, c'est Christian. Je peux aller jouer dehors avec lui ?

Elle a hoché la tête, tout en essayant de rester entre son père et son mari.

— Oui oui…

Je suis allé rejoindre Christian, et une fois dehors, j'ai enfin pu rigoler aussi fort que j'en avais envie. Je m'é-

tais tellement retenu que ça a duré
un moment. Christian me regardait
de son air un peu ahuri.

— Il se passe toujours des tas de
trucs bizarres chez vous, il a dit.

Sans ajouter un mot, je l'ai
entraîné, et on est revenus se glisser
sous la fenêtre de la cuisine, discrètement, en se courbant. Là, on a écouté
la suite de la conversation.

— Faites-moi plaisir, demandait
papa, dites-moi que vous avez au moins
un peu participé.

Pas dégonflé, pépé a rétorqué :

— Ah, mais ça oui, parfaitement !
J'ai payé le jus de fruit du gamin ! Et je

43

peux vous dire que c'était pas donné !

— Ah ! Tu vois, Robert ! a fait maman.

Je n'ai pas pu tenir, j'avais tellement envie de rire qu'il a fallu qu'on déguerpisse ; on allait se faire repérer, sinon. Un peu plus loin dans la rue, Christian, un peu agacé, m'a demandé :

— Mais qu'est-ce qui s'est passé, à la fin ?

— Hi hi hi... Attends que je t'explique... Ha ha ha...

Je lui ai raconté et il a été épaté.

— Tout ça parce que ton pépé n'a pas aimé le potiron d'hier soir !

— Oui ! Ça se passe souvent comme ça chez moi !

Et je lui ai fait signe de se taire parce que maman venait de sortir de la maison. Elle essayait d'entraîner papa dans le jardin, histoire de lui faire prendre l'air et de le détendre. On l'a entendu dire :

— Allez, Robert, calme-toi, maintenant !

Et papa de répondre :

— Je suis calme, Marie-Rose. Ruiné, mais calme.

Moi, en tout cas, je n'avais jamais aussi bien mangé ! Ah, je m'en souviendrai du repas de pépé ; et papa aussi ! Mais pas pour les mêmes raisons. Mon pépé, il a vraiment un caractère de cochon, mais au moins, avec lui, on rigole bien. Et c'est super important de pouvoir rire aux éclats, quand on a huit ans !

2

Capricieuse Caprice

Qu'est-ce que c'est compliqué, les filles ! Ces derniers temps, pourtant, je nageais dans le bonheur avec Chen ! Après l'école, on faisait de longues promenades romantiques, on s'achetait des glaces aux mille parfums, on allait au cinéma voir de chouettes films… La belle vie, quoi !

On ne se quittait plus, elle et moi. Et j'étais tout près de lui dire ce qu'elle voulait entendre depuis toujours : que je l'aime pour la vie et que rien, jamais, ne pourra nous séparer…

Le problème, c'est que côté école, ce n'était pas terrible ! Je n'arrivais pas à aimer l'école autant que Chen. Pour tout dire, je ne me voyais pas passer toute ma vie à l'école ; alors qu'avec Chen, ça me paraissait tout à fait possible. Même mes copains, je les voyais de moins en moins.

Alors, lorsque je suis tombé un jour sur Christian, assis dans l'herbe du parc, j'ai été plutôt content.

— Salut, Christian ! Ça faisait longtemps, dis donc !

Il a vaguement levé la main et a agité le bout des doigts, mais je voyais bien qu'il n'était pas dans son assiette. Je me suis allongé à coté de lui et je me suis inquiété :

— T'en fais une drôle de tête !!! Qu'est-ce qui t'arrive ?

Derrière ses grosses lunettes, il semblait avoir les paupières toutes molles.

Il a levé vers moi des yeux de chien battu et a fait :

— Tu vas pas me croire, vieux : je suis amoureux !

C'était la meilleure ! Christian amoureux ! Lui qui a toujours considéré les filles comme des plantes d'ornement ! J'en ai été tout épaté et je lui ai rétorqué :

— C'est fou ça ! Je croyais que tu t'intéressais pas aux filles ! Eh ben allez, dis... C'est qui ? hein...

Il a ouvert la bouche, mais avant

qu'il ait prononcé un mot, je l'ai interrompu :

— Attends, laisse-moi deviner, ça doit être... euh... Pas Julie, elle est trop foldingue, pas Linda, elle est trop tarte...

Je n'ai pas eu le temps de continuer ; derrière nous a retenti un bruit régulier et saccadé, comme une machine qui soufflait à intervalles réguliers :

— Pfff... Pfff... Pfff...

On s'est retournés et on a vu passer Caprice qui faisait son jogging dans l'allée, comme tous les

jours. Elle nous a lancé un sourire éblouissant.

— Pfff… Bonjour, Cédric ! Pfff… Pfff… Bonjour, Christian !

Je l'ai saluée :

— 'Jour, Caprice !

Et puis mes yeux sont retombés sur Christian. Il était devenu rouge comme un jus de tomate, il avait le menton qui tombait et les verres de ses lunettes s'étaient couverts de buée.

Alors, la mémoire m'est revenue, et
je me suis tordu de rire.

— WHAA HAHA HA !!! Mais c'est
vrai ! J'avais oublié ! C'est Caprice !
T'es amoureux de Caprice ! WHAA
HAHA HA !!!

Il a pris un air mauvais, en disant :

— Je vois pas ce qu'il y a de drôle !

— Bien, il va juste falloir que tu
travailles ton sprint… WHAA HAHA
HA !!!

Il était trop marrant, Christian :

pour rattraper Caprice, il allait devoir louer une mobylette !

Quand j'ai réussi à me calmer, j'ai essayé de comprendre :

— Mais au fait, je croyais que ça t'avait passé, ton béguin pour Caprice ?!

Christian a haussé les épaules, avec une expression à la fois rêveuse et très fatiguée.

— Ben moi aussi, je croyais. Mais

pas du tout. Et cette fois, c'est vraiment sérieux ; je ressens exactement ce que tu m'avais dit pour toi avec Chen.

J'étais curieux de savoir ce qu'il voulait dire par là.

— Ah bon ? ai-je fait.

— Oui ! Quand elle est près de moi, mon cœur se met à battre fort, aussi vite qu'un cheval au galop ! J'ai chaud partout, je transpire, alors que je ne cours même pas ! Et

puis tout de suite après, j'ai froid, froid comme quand j'ai la grippe. Mais surtout, je me sens léger comme si j'étais en train de voler, et heureux, tu peux pas savoir !

J'ai hoché la tête, l'air du gars qui est déjà passé par là.

— Si si, je peux. Et quand elle est loin de toi, tu te demandes où elle est, si elle ne t'a pas oublié, et si elle ne compte pas te laisser tomber comme une vieille chaussette.

— Oui, voilà. Et je me sens malheureux, mais malheureux ! C'est affreux.

Pas de doute, ma longue expérience ne pouvait pas me tromper : Christian était gravement amoureux. Le pauvre, il allait drôlement en baver ! Mais ça, j'ai préféré ne pas lui dire tout de suite. Il y avait juste un détail que je voulais connaître ; je lui ai demandé :

— Mais au fait, Caprice, elle, elle est amoureuse de toi ?

Christian a froncé les sourcils en me regardant, comme si j'avais eu une panne de cerveau.

— Évidemment, grosse banane ! Seulement elle ose pas me le dire... Parce qu'elle n'est pas sûre que je l'aime, moi aussi... Bref, c'est l'impasse !

Je me suis gratté la tête en réfléchissant. Qu'est-ce que j'allais bien pouvoir inventer pour l'aider ? Alors je me suis souvenu de ce que pépé m'avait dit, quelques jours plus tôt.

— Écoute, vieux, ce qu'il faut, c'est que t'assures… Si t'es amoureux, c'est que t'es plus un gamin, mais un homme, tu comprends ?

— Ah bon…

— Alors il faut que t'en aies l'air. Les filles, elles adorent ça !

Christian s'est redressé en gonflant un peu la poitrine.

— D'accord, mais comment faut faire pour avoir l'air d'un homme ? a-t-il dit en essayant de prendre une voix plus grave.

— Pépé, il prétend qu'on devient un homme quand on a du poil au menton. Christian a aussitôt passé ses doigts sur ses joues, mais c'était aussi doux que des fesses de bébé.

— Bon ben alors, il a lancé, c'est pas demain la veille !

Mais je n'avais pas fini :

— Attends ! Le principal, c'est pas de devenir un homme du jour au lendemain ; c'est juste d'en avoir l'air ! Pépé m'a confié un truc génial qu'il faisait quand il était jeune.

— Et c'est quoi ? a demandé Christian qui ne me croyait qu'à moitié.

Je le lui ai glissé à l'oreille, en

chuchotant pour que le secret ne s'envole pas :

— Tu te colles un sparadrap là, sur la joue, et hop ! Les filles pensent que tu t'es coupé en te rasant. Ça marche à tous les coups !

Il a fait la moue, pas l'air convaincu du tout :

— À tous les coups, à tous les coups… Je préfère que tu essaies toi-même… Comme ça, je verrai si ça marche.

On s'est tapé dans la main, en se donnant rendez-vous le lendemain à la première heure. Au petit matin,

Christian m'attendait devant chez moi ; il m'a aidé à me coller sur la joue deux bandes de sparadrap que j'avais piquées dans l'armoire à pharmacie de la salle de bain. On a fait la route ensemble jusqu'à l'école.

En franchissant les grilles, juste avant de rentrer dans la cour, je lui ai demandé à voix basse :

— Bon, t'as bien compris ce que tu devais dire ?

— T'inquiète !

Et il a tout de suite commencé à jouer son rôle. En arrivant dans la cour, il m'a désigné du doigt et il a lancé, très fort :

— BEN, CÉDRIC ! QU'EST-CE QUE TU T'ES FAIT, LÀ ?

J'ai joué l'innocent :

— Hein ? Où ça ?

— BEN LÀ ! SUR LA JOUE !

Autour de nous, les copains se sont immobilisés et leurs conversations se sont arrêtées. J'ai porté la main à ma pommette et j'ai tapoté délicatement mon pansement.

— Oh, ça ? C'est rien, je me suis un peu coupé ce matin en me rasant !

— BEN MINCE ALORS ! a poursuivi Christian en forçant toujours la voix ; EH ! VENEZ VOIR, CÉDRIC S'EST COUPÉ CE MATIN EN SE RASANT !

Un attroupement s'est aussitôt
formé autour de moi, et Christian a
dû s'en rendre compte, il y avait
plus de filles que de garçons ! Et
impressionnées, les filles ! Mais il
fallait que je reste modeste : j'ai
légèrement soulevé les épaules et
j'ai dit, comme pour m'excuser :

— Ben oui, qu'est-ce que vous
voulez, on vieillit ! Les corvées com-
mencent !

Tout le monde s'est mis à mur-
murer et les filles ont poussé des
petits rires. J'ai discrètement lancé
un clin d'œil à Christian ; mainte-

nant, il avait la preuve que ça marchait, mon truc ! Et puis Félix, un gars de la classe à qui on n'avait rien demandé, s'en est mêlé. Il a cherché à me coincer :

— Dis donc, Cédric, il est de quelle marque, ton rasoir ?

Si je m'attendais à un truc comme ça ! Franchement, je n'avais pas du tout pensé à ce genre de détail. J'ai essayé de me dépatouiller comme j'ai pu :

— Ben c'est un … Heu .. un … un « raz »… un « raz »…

— Un « Razplus », comme celui de mon père ?

Sans le savoir, il me tirait d'affaire. J'ai sauté sur l'occasion :

— Euh voilà, oui, un « Razplus » : exactement, ça me revient… C'est un « Razplus » !

Mais il a fait une tête bizarre et tout le monde l'a regardé. Il a fini par constater :

— C'est bizarre.

Il commençait à me chauffer les doigts de pieds, cet énergumène.

— Quoi ? Qu'est-ce qu'il y a de bizarre ? j'ai dit.

— Ben je me demande juste comment t'as fait pour te couper avec un rasoir électrique...

La honte du siècle. La déculottée. La catastrophe. Je m'étais trahi et une explosion de rires a retenti dans la cour, tout autour de moi. Ce qui

m'a fait le plus mal, c'est de voir à quel point Chen riait de bon cœur, et Sophie aussi, et Adeline, et toutes les autres. Sans parler de Nicolas qui s'est à moitié étranglé. Il n'y a que Christian qui ne riait pas. Je suis vite allé me débarrasser des sparadraps dans une poubelle et j'ai préféré dire à Mlle Nelly que j'avais mal à la tête ; comme ça, je suis resté dans la classe à la récré.

Il fallait le reconnaître : mon idée avait échoué, mon plan était nul. J'ai passé une très mauvaise journée, et le soir même, quand je suis rentré à la maison, pépé en a entendu de toutes les couleurs.

— Au fait, bravo, pépé, pour l'histoire des pansements sur les joues !

— Pourquoi, ça a raté ?

— Complètement, oui ! Je n'ai jamais été aussi ridicule ! Merci quand même !

Enfin, ça avait au moins montré à

Christian que l'amour n'était pas qu'une partie de plaisir : lui aussi, il n'en était qu'au début de ses contrariétés. Il était loin de se douter de toutes les douleurs qu'il allait encore devoir supporter ! Heureusement pour lui, il m'avait comme copain. Et malgré cet épisode un peu lamentable, il pourrait encore compter sur moi...

Dès le lendemain après-midi, je l'ai retrouvé là où il passait le plus clair de son temps : dans le parc, au bord de l'allée qui servait de piste de course à Caprice. Je me suis assis à côté de lui et, ensemble, on a compté le nombre de fois où notre championne passait devant nous. Le problème, c'est qu'elle ne semblait toujours pas fatiguée et courait toujours aussi vite. J'ai posé ma main sur l'épaule de Christian en lui disant :

— Allez, vieux, fais pas cette tête,

elle finira pas bien par être essouf-
flée !

— J'y crois plus : ça fait une heure
qu'elle tourne !

Il était désespéré. Je devais intervenir sans tarder.

— De toute façon, le seul moyen
de sortir de l'impasse, c'est de te
déclarer, comme ça, direct !

Christian a secoué la tête.

— Facile à dire ! Même toi, tu n'y
es jamais arrivé avec Chen…

Je ne voyais pas le rapport. Et puis
je suis toujours un peu chatouilleux

lorsqu'on aborde ce sujet. J'ai senti mes poings se serrer.

— Oui, bon ben là, c'est de toi qu'on parle ! Et de personne d'autre ! Chen et moi, ça n'a rien à voir ! D'accord !

— Bon, te fâche pas ! a fait Christian en se reculant ; mais qu'est-ce que tu veux que je lui déclare ?

— Ben la vérité ! Que tu l'aimes comme un fou, qu'elle est ton rêve d'Asie, ta perle de riz, ton lotus des rizières !

— Euh… là, tu confonds, il me semble ; Caprice, elle vient d'Afrique, elle !

Quel idiot, ce Christian ! Toujours la réflexion qui tue, la remarque bête !

— Et alors ? Quelle importance ? Tu improvises, c'est tout ! L'amour, le vrai, ça n'a rien à voir avec la géographie, tout de même !

Mais il était buté.

— De toute façon, je trouverai jamais les mots.

Connaissant un peu Christian, il n'avait pas tort de penser ça. Mais il y avait un moyen de s'en sortir :

— Alors tu dis rien, si t'as peur de sortir une bêtise ! Mais dans ce cas-là, tu changes de méthode : tu lui offres quelque chose pour lui prouver ton amour.

On s'est interrompus un moment parce que Caprice repassait et on a regardé s'éloigner sa silhouette

élancée. Christian a fini par secouer la tête et a soupiré, en cherchant quelque chose dans sa poche :

— Justement, je voulais lui offrir ça. Pour qu'elle pense à moi, entre deux courses.

Il m'a tendu une photo de lui, un peu froissée, sur laquelle il n'avait pas l'air plus malin que d'habitude. Mais je ne lui ai pas dit. Il se grattait la tête, mal à l'aise.

— Tu comprends, a-t-il alors gémi.

Pour lui donner, il faudrait que j'arrive à la rattraper. Mais il me faut du temps !

— Te décourage pas, vieux ! Insiste ! Elle va bientôt revenir ; va te mettre près de la piste et tends-lui ta photo au passage.

— Ouais, t'as raison, je vais essayer.

Il s'est levé et a trottiné sur la pelouse jusqu'au bord de l'allée.

Mais il avait mal calculé son coup et il est arrivé un poil trop tard. Comme une fusée, Caprice a déboulé de derrière un fourré et lui est passée devant. Avant qu'elle disparaisse, il a juste eu le temps de lever la main et de dire :

— Cap...

Le reste s'est perdu dans les arbres. En plus, Christian s'est pris un petit caillou dans l'œil. Je sais que ce n'est pas bien de se moquer, mais cette fois, je n'ai pas pu me retenir :

— WAAARF ! WAAARF ! WAAARF ! Laisse pas tomber, vieux, elle va revenir !

Il était tellement énervé qu'on aurait presque pu voir de la fumée sortir de ses oreilles. Mais il est têtu, Christian, et en amour, souvent, ça sert d'être têtu. Il est resté planté au bord de l'allée, et quand Caprice s'est approchée, au tour suivant, il s'est carrément mis au milieu de son chemin. Il a fait :

— Hé, Caprice !

Du coup, elle a bien été obligée de s'arrêter. Mais pour ne pas perdre le rythme, elle a continué à courir en faisant du surplace.

— Pfffh Pffffh pffhh ! Oui, Christian ? Pfffhh… Pfffhhh… Je t'écoute.

Tu parles qu'elle l'écoutait ! Elle a même commencé à faire une série d'assouplissements, en gardant les jambes droites et en touchant le sol du bout des doigts. Christian ne savait plus comment la regarder, elle bougeait la tête sans arrêt.

— Tiens, regarde ! a-t-il fini par dire.

Et il lui a tendu sa photo. Là, enfin, elle s'est immobilisée, surprise, mais plutôt souriante. Elle a soulevé les sourcils, hoché plusieurs fois la tête et puis a rendu la photo à Christian en disant :

— Ooh mais… C'est une très jolie photo, Christian ! Garde-la précieusement !

Et elle est repartic sans se

retourner. Je n'en pouvais plus. J'ai ri si fort que tous les oiseaux, dans les arbres alentours, ont préféré changer de perchoir.

— WAAARF ! WAAARF ! WAAARF ! Aaaah, c'est trop... J'y crois pas !

Après un moment, je me suis quand même un peu calmé et je suis retourné vers lui, en m'essuyant les yeux.

— Allez, Christian, tu vas tout de même pas te laisser abattre si facilement !

— OH TOI, ÇA VA, HEIN !

Il était furax. Il commençait seulement à comprendre que sa vie d'amoureux, avant d'arriver à un vrai résultat, serait une longue succession d'échecs. Et que les filles, elles ne font jamais ce qu'on croit qu'elles vont faire.

De rage, il s'est mis à déchirer sa photo en mille morceaux et il a jeté les confettis en l'air, par-dessus son épaule. Le problème, c'est qu'un coup de vent a emporté les débris au milieu de l'allée, juste au moment ou Caprice repassait. Elle en a aspiré un bon paquet, et ce n'est jamais agréable de respirer des bouts de papier quand on essaie de battre des records d'endurance. Elle s'est mise à étouffer et a dû s'arrêter, pliée en deux par une énorme quinte de toux bien grasse.

— KOOF ! KOOF ! KOOF !

Des copines se sont aussitôt précipitées vers elle et l'ont soutenue, pendant qu'elle recrachait les morceaux

de la photo de Christian. L'une d'elle l'a même enguirlandée, en lui tapant dans le dos :

— Je te l'avais dit, qu'à force de courir la bouche ouverte, tu finirais par avaler n'importe quoi !

On est restés un peu à l'écart, Christian et moi, en espérant que les morceaux seraient trop petits pour qu'on puisse le reconnaître. Je n'ai pas pu m'empêcher de remarquer, en chuchotant :

— Tu vois, elle a fini par l'avoir ta photo ! Bon, évidemment, t'avais pas prévu qu'elle la mange : mais c'est déjà ça, non ?

— Ah toi, n'en rajoute pas, hein !
a-t-il dit sur le même ton. Ou je te
déchire aussi en mille morceaux !

Et on s'est éclipsés discrètement.
Pauvre Christian ! Vraiment, c'est pas
son truc, les filles ! Mais je le reconnais,
j'aurais pas dû me moquer de lui. Du
coup, j'ai voulu me racheter. Comme il
m'avait promis de déclarer son amour
à Caprice, mais qu'il lui fallait du
temps, j'ai organisé une sorte de
rendez-vous pour le mercredi suivant.
Là, il aurait tout son après-midi.

On s'est rendus dans le parc après
déjeuner. À une heure et demie,
Caprice était déjà là, bondissante
comme une panthère. Christian en a
été épaté :

— Mince alors ! a-t-il soufflé ; comment t'as fait ?

— Fastoche ! Je lui ai téléphoné en déguisant ma voix et je me suis fait passer pour le prof de gym. Je lui ai dit que le directeur d'un club d'athlétisme l'avait remarquée ! Et qu'elle devait venir s'entraîner aujourd'hui parce que lui, c'était son seul après-midi de libre !

— Ben toi, alors !

Eh oui ! Le courage et les idées audacieuses, c'était ma spécialité. Lui, il était plutôt du genre à traîner des pieds ; Caprice était là, à peine à vingt mètres et il n'osait toujours pas y aller. Il s'était caché derrière un gros chêne. Quel gamin ! J'ai essayé de le secouer en l'attrapant par les épaules :

— Bon ben t'y vas ? Qu'est-ce que t'attends ?

Il a enroulé ses bras autour de l'arbre derrière lequel il était caché.

— Me pousse pas, non plus ! a-t-il râlé. Il était accroché au tronc comme à une bouée de sauvetage.

Qu'est-ce qu'il m'énervait !

— Sois un homme, quoi ! Ou alors c'est pas la peine que je me décarcasse !

— Je suis désolé, mais j'y arrive pas ! J'ai pas ton expérience, moi !

Et puis je l'ai senti se relâcher. Il avait remarqué que quelqu'un arrivait et son regard s'est radouci. Il a dit, en me faisant un clin d'œil :

— Tiens, v'là Chen !

Je me suis retourné. Ma petite porcelaine transparente de Chine impériale descendait l'allée, belle comme une cascade d'eau fraîche se jetant dans le Yang-Tsé. Apparemment, son apparition faisait réfléchir Christian. Il s'est mordillé les lèvres avant de proposer :

— Écoute, j'ai une idée ! Tu fais ta déclaration à Chen et moi j'écoute comment tu t'y prends.

J'ai senti le sol mollir sous mes

pieds et soudain l'air m'a manqué. Je m'attendais à tout sauf à ça.

— Co... Comment je m'y prends ? ai-je bégayé. Et pourquoi moi ? Ça va pas la tête, non ?

Chen venait de nous apercevoir ; elle s'est arrêtée pour nous faire un petit coucou. C'était gentil à elle.

— Oh, bonjour, Cédric ! Bonjour, Christian !

J'ai levé la main pour lui répondre, mais je me sentais plutôt gêné. D'autant que Caprice, à quelques mètres de là, trottinait toujours sur place, en soufflant régulièrement.

— Heu... bonjour, Chen... Je... Heu... tu tombes bien, parce que...

J'avais beau prendre ma phrase par tous les bouts, je n'arrivais pas à m'en dépêtrer. Chen m'a gentiment donné

un coup de main :

— Qu'est ce que vous faisiez ?

M'avançant vers d'elle, je lui ai glissé :

— Oh euh… C'est à cause de Christian. Il a un problème de… comment dire… Un problème d'homme, si tu vois ce que je veux dire. Alors je m'occupe de lui.

Elle a souri et ses yeux sont devenus deux filets d'or.

— C'est gentil, ça, d'aider un ami. Mais quel genre de problème ?

Elle venait de poser la bonne question. Elle était peut-être là, la solution. Ça n'allait sûrement pas faire très plaisir à Christian, mais au moins, moi, ça me retirait une belle épine du pied.

— En fait, hmm… voilà : il est amoureux. Amoureux de Caprice. Mais tu comprends, il n'ose pas le lui dire et… ça le rend très malheureux. Tu voudrais pas nous…

— Bien sûr, y'a pas de problème, les garçons !

Christian avait entendu. Il m'a fait des gestes désespérés, les yeux roulants derrière les verres ronds de ses lunettes, comme des poissons affolés dans leur aquarium. Il a gémi :

— M'enfin, mais t'es fou ! Qu'est-ce que tu lui as dit ?

Chen avait bien compris le message. Déjà, elle se dirigeait vers Caprice. Alors Christian a fait sa crise de nerfs. Il est sorti de derrière le chêne en hurlant et en gesticulant comme s'il avait été saupoudré de poil à gratter.

— NON, C'EST PAS VRAI ! C'EST CÉDRIC QU'A TOUT INVENTÉ ! LE PROF DE GYM, LE RENDEZ-

VOUS, TOUT !

Un gros silence est tombé sur le parc. On s'est regardés les uns les autres pendant un moment et puis Chen a explosé la première:

— CÉDRIC ! COMMENT PEUX-TU FAIRE UNE CHOSE PAREILLE À TON MEILLEUR AMI !!! C'EST UNE HONTE !!!

Elle s'est plantée devant moi et m'a envoyé une baffe à déraciner un cocotier. Après ça, Caprice est arrivée à grandes enjambées et a crié :

— ALORS LE PROF DE GYM,

C'ÉTAIT TOI ? EH BIEN C'EST PAS DRÔLE DU TOUT !? ET TIENS, ÇA T'APPRENDRA !

À son tour, elle a pris son élan et m'a donné une énorme claque sur l'autre joue. J'avais l'impression d'avoir été heurté par une double locomotive lancée à pleine vitesse. Je me suis retenu de pleurer, parce que j'aurais eu la honte, mais ce n'est pas l'envie qui m'en manquait. En serrant les dents, j'ai attendu que les deux filles s'éloignent et je me suis tourné vers Christian.

— TU T'ES DÉGONFLÉ, HEIN !!! ESPÈCE DE TRAÎTRE !!!

Il était aussi énervé que moi. Peut-être même encore plus. Je l'ai vu fermer les poings et serrer les mâchoires.

— C'EST TOI LE TRAÎTRE ! ET JE VAIS TE…

Il s'est jeté sur moi sans prendre le temps de terminer sa phrase et m'a attrapé au col. Avant de se taper dessus, on a encore eu le temps de parlementer un peu :

— FAUX DERCHE ! DÉGONFLÉ ! MINABLE !

— TRAÎTRE !!! FRIMEUR !!! CAFTEUR !!!

Après, je ne me souviens plus de grand-chose, sauf qu'on a essayé de se faire mal, et qu'on y est assez bien arrivé. Mais tout ça n'a pas duré longtemps, parce qu'on s'est vite rendu compte que ça ne servait à rien de se battre. Alors, on s'est arrêtés et on s'est mis à compter nos bosses.

— Tu veux que je te dise, Christian ? Tout ça, c'est à cause des filles…

Il s'est tamponné une égratignure que je lui avais faite sur le nez et il a remarqué :

— Ouais, et je sais pas toi, mais moi, je ne suis pas prêt de m'y laisser reprendre. Les filles sont bien trop compliquées. Et puis Caprice, elle court bien trop vite pour moi…

C'est vrai que c'est un manque de chance pour Christian d'être devenu gaga d'une championne de course à pied. Moi, j'ai plus de veine. Et au moins, je suis sûr que Chen est amoureuse de moi. Ça fait toute la différence. J'en suis sûr parce que si elle ne m'aimait pas, elle ne se fâcherait pas contre moi quand je la déçois. N'empêche qu'elle tape fort.

Ah, il n'a pas tort, Christian ; à huit ans, les filles sont vraiment trop compliquées !

Table

1. Dîner-surprise 5

2. Capricieuse Caprice 47

The Perfect Kitten

Pet Rescue Adventures:

Max the Missing Puppy

Ginger the Stray Kitten

Buttons the Runaway Puppy

The Frightened Kitten

Jessie the Lonely Puppy

The Kitten Nobody Wanted

Harry the Homeless Puppy

Lost in the Snow

Leo All Alone

The Brave Kitten

The Secret Puppy

Sky the Unwanted Kitten

Misty the Abandoned Kitten

The Scruffy Puppy

The Lost Puppy

The Missing Kitten

The Secret Kitten

The Rescued Puppy

Sammy the Shy Kitten

The Tiniest Puppy

Alone in the Night

Lost in the Storm

Teddy in Trouble

A Home for Sandy

The Curious Kitten

The Abandoned Puppy

The Sad Puppy

The Homeless Kitten

The Stolen Kitten

The Forgotten Puppy

The Homesick Puppy

A Kitten Named Tiger

The Puppy Who Was Left Behind

The Kidnapped Kitten

The Seaside Puppy

The Rescued Kitten

Oscar's Lonely Christmas

The Unwanted Puppy

Also by Holly Webb:

Little Puppy Lost

The Snow Bear

The Perfect Kitten

by Holly Webb
Illustrated by Sophy Williams

tiger tales

tiger tales

5 River Road, Suite 128, Wilton, CT 06897
Published in the United States 2019
Originally published in Great Britain 2019
by the Little Tiger Group
Text copyright © 2019 Holly Webb
Illustrations copyright © 2019 Sophy Williams
Author photograph copyright Nigel Bird
ISBN-13: 978-1-68010-447-9
ISBN-10: 1-68010-447-0
Printed in China
STP/1800/0261/0319
All rights reserved
10 9 8 7 6 5 4 3 2 1

For more insight and activities, visit us at www.tigertalesbooks.com

Contents

Chapter One
Exciting News 7

Chapter Two
Kittens! 23

Chapter Three
A Special Meeting 36

Chapter Four
Settling In 52

Chapter Five
A Fun Game 72

Chapter Six
Missing! 87

Chapter Seven
A Clever Idea 100

Chapter Eight
Home Again 115

For all the brave, loving people who adopt an animal that isn't "perfect"

Chapter One
Exciting News

Abi stared at her mom and stepdad, her mouth hanging open. The cereal and milk slid off her spoon, and her little sister, Ruby, giggled. "Look what you're doing!" she said.

"Do you really mean it?" Abi asked her mom. "You're not joking?"

Her mom and stepdad grinned at each other.

"Of course we mean it," Abi's mom said. "We're absolutely serious!"

"Oooh, your milk's going everywhere," Ruby said, and Abi quickly put the spoon back in her bowl.

"Didn't you hear what Mom just said?" she asked her sister, and when Ruby looked confused, she told her, "We can get a cat!"

"Today?" asked Ruby hopefully. Ruby was only four, and she didn't like waiting for things to happen.

Abi looked doubtfully at her mom

and stepdad. She had a feeling that getting a cat would take a while, especially if they were going to an animal rescue to find one.

"No, Ruby, not today," Chris, Abi's stepdad, said gently. "But we can look at photos of the cats we might get on the computer. There's an animal rescue not far from here, Linfield Cats and Dogs. They put photos of the animals that need homes on their website."

"I want a cat *now*." Ruby sighed, and her nose wrinkled the way it did when she was about to get upset.

"If you finish your breakfast, we could look at the pictures now," Mom suggested, and Ruby nodded and started to eat her cereal very fast.

Abi looked at her bowl—she'd almost

finished anyway, and she was too excited to eat any more. She'd been trying to persuade her mom and Chris that they should get a cat for such a long time. They'd always said Ruby was too little and she might chase a cat or try to push it around in her toy stroller. Abi had tried telling them she'd watch Ruby like a hawk and make sure she didn't do anything so silly, but they'd always said no—until today.

"Are there a lot of cats on the website?" she asked, and Chris nodded.

"Yes! I took a quick look yesterday. There were so many."

"Oh, wow…," Abi muttered, clenching her fingers into her palms. She wanted to bounce up from the table and look at the photos right away.

What kinds of cats would there be? she wondered. And what cat would she like, if she had a choice?

Black cats were beautiful and mysterious, and she loved it when they had little white paws. Or maybe they could get a tabby—all those beautiful stripes. Then again, what about a tortoiseshell? Her friend Sky from school had a tortoiseshell named Wanda who was white with orange and black splashes, and one orange ear and one black ear. Even her whiskers were white on one side and black on the other. Wanda was the cutest cat Abi had ever seen.

In the end, Abi decided she didn't mind. A cat of their own would be wonderful whatever color it was, as long as it was friendly and didn't mind being petted. Maybe it would even sleep on her bed, or take turns between her bed and Ruby's.

"Are you almost done?" she asked Ruby hopefully. She watched as her sister chased the last bit of cereal around her bowl. As soon as she had finished, Abi jumped up eagerly.

"Let's all go and sit on the couch," Mom suggested. "Chris, if you bring your laptop over, we can look at the cats together."

Abi's stepdad went to get the computer, and they all snuggled up on the couch. Ruby climbed onto Abi's lap, and Abi peered around her at the screen.

"Are you all right like that?" Mom asked doubtfully, and Abi nodded.

She was a bit squished, but she didn't mind, since Ruby was so cuddly. Soon it might be Ruby *and* a cat sitting on her!

"Oh, look...," Abi whispered, and Ruby reached out to pat the screen. Staring out at them was a black cat with round green eyes, like marbles.

"Her name is Nala," Chris said. "What a beauty."

"I want that cat," Ruby announced.

"She's beautiful," Mom agreed. "But don't you think we should look at *all* the cats before we decide? And I'm afraid it says Nala needs a home without young children because she's a little nervous."

Abi sighed, but she understood why they couldn't adopt Nala. A nervous cat probably wasn't going to enjoy being loved by Ruby. They needed a super friendly cat. "Let's look at some more, Ruby. Oh, wow, kittens!"

"Kittens!" Ruby and Mom echoed together, and Chris laughed. "They're very cute!"

The black kittens were curled up together in a basket, staring up at the camera. They looked surprised, as if the flash had woken them up.

"Aren't they fluffy?" Abi said. She

14

hadn't even thought about getting a long-haired cat. This was so exciting! "I'm not sure how we'll ever choose…," she said to Mom. "I want all of them."

"I know." Her mom laughed. "Once we've registered with the rescue center, they'll come over for a home visit to check that we're a good home for a cat. Maybe they can suggest some cats that will be just right for us." Then she shook her head. "I should have said that the other way around. Some cats that *we'll* be just right for!"

Abi nodded and smiled. It was the nicest thought. There was a beautiful cat waiting for them at the animal rescue, and they would be the perfect home for it.

"Mom, do you think it's okay for Ruby to be here?" Abi whispered, watching her little sister trailing a doll along the floor by her hair. The volunteer from the animal rescue was due to arrive any minute, and Abi wanted everything to be just right. She had been worrying about the visit ever since Mom had registered with the rescue the previous weekend.

"What do you mean?" Mom gave her a confused look.

"Just ... maybe Chris could take her to the park? What if the people from the animal rescue think she's too

16

little to have a cat?" Ruby had been so excited all week, but there was a chance that she might come across as really silly....

Mom smiled at her. "It's okay, Abi. We said we're interested in adopting a cat that would be happy around a younger child, so we don't need to pretend that we don't have Ruby. And we want to get a cat that will actually *like* living here. I think children aged nine and four should be fine for most cats."

"Yes ... we cleaned up, though," Abi pointed out. "To make us look like better cat owners. Isn't that the same thing?"

"No, it isn't!" Mom looked around at the unusually clean kitchen. "But I know what you mean. I don't think cats care about mess. It's the people from the animal rescue who I was cleaning up for."

"They're here!" Abi jumped as the bell rang and Ruby rushed to answer it. Luckily Chris got there first, and then Ruby went suddenly shy as she saw a strange woman on the doorstep and hid behind his legs.

"Hi! Come in—would you like some tea?" Mom asked.

But the woman—the name tag on her red fleece said Maria—didn't come any farther in, even though Chris was holding the door open for her. She was standing just inside the gate, watching the street and looking rather worried. Then she turned to them and smiled anxiously.

"I'm really sorry…," she started to say, and then glanced down at her feet as though she didn't know quite how to go on. "It's our fault. I should have realized before I came out to see you…. I didn't check the address."

"What is it?" Chris asked, frowning. "Is there a problem?"

Abi slipped her hand into Mom's.

She wasn't sure what was going on, but she could tell it wasn't good.

"It's your street," Maria explained. "It's so busy. There are a few main roads through town that are a problem, and this is one of them. We placed a cat with a family near here last year, and she was hit by a car. After that, we decided we wouldn't let anyone along this road take one of our cats. It's just too dangerous."

"I don't think our road's that busy," Abi said stubbornly to Mom. Chris had taken Ruby out to buy some bread for lunch, but it was mostly to give them something to do. Ruby didn't understand why Maria hadn't stayed to look around the house or why they weren't getting a cat now, and she kept asking about it.

"I suppose we're used to the road." Mom sighed. "I didn't think it was busy, either, until she said. But she's right."

"Cats are clever, though—I bet it would be okay. Couldn't we just go to another animal rescue and see if the people there don't mind about the road?"

"We *could*.... But remember what Maria said about it being really difficult for cats to judge how fast cars are going, especially in the evening when it's getting dark? That's when they're most likely to get hurt." Mom turned around and gave Abi a hug.

"I know it doesn't seem fair. I'm sad about it, too. But what if we did get a cat and we all fell in love with her and then she got hurt? Wouldn't that be worse than not having a cat at all?"

"No," Abi said crossly. She knew Mom was right, really—but it didn't mean she had to like it.

Chapter Two
Kittens!

"When are you getting your cat?" Sky asked, grabbing at Abi's hands. She had dashed over to Abi as soon as she saw her come into the playground, wanting to hear her cat news. Abi had told Sky they were having a visit from the animal rescue, and she was almost as excited about Abi getting a cat as Abi was.

Abi made a face. "We aren't. The

rescue said our street is too busy—they can't let us have one."

Sky stared at her. "No! I didn't even know they could do that. What did your mom and Chris say?"

"That the rescue is right." Abi sighed. "And I know they are, really, but I was so happy, thinking we were going to have a cat at last. You're so lucky to live on a quiet street."

"I've never even thought about it," Sky said. "Wanda goes out all the time. But there are people on your street who have cats, aren't there?"

"Yeah. I suppose their cats are just really careful. And they haven't come from rescue centers." Abi slumped down on a bench. "I was so excited...."

"It doesn't seem fair." Sky sat down and put her arm around Abi's shoulders. "You'd be such a good cat owner. Wanda loves it when you come over."

"Mom suggested we get some fish." Abi shook her head. "It just isn't the same thing."

"You can't pet a fish," Sky agreed. "What about a dog?"

"Nope. Mom thinks we're all too busy to manage the walks and everything.

And I like dogs, but not the same way that I love cats." She giggled. "Chris said maybe we should get a lizard, and Ruby thought that was a great idea. I've never seen Mom look so worried." Then her smile faded, and she looked miserably at Sky. "I don't see how we can ever get a cat—not unless we move to a new house."

"Look at these—oh, little sweethearts!" Maria peered into the box. "They're tiny. Maybe six weeks, do you think? They're early. We haven't hit kitten season yet!"

The three kittens peered back up at her cautiously, eyes round and wary.

There was nothing else in the box with them, not even an old towel, and they were huddled close together. Their mother was gone, and they were cold and scared.

"Where did they come from?" Lily asked, coming to look. "Wow, they *are* pretty. Beautiful striped tabbies—and we don't often get a pure white kitten."

Maria picked up the white kitten gently. "She's a girl. Isn't she sweet? And what blue eyes! They were left behind the garbage cans outside the supermarket. One of the workers from the warehouse brought them in. He said he wished he could keep them, but he didn't think they'd like his dog."

"At least they weren't dumped until they started eating solid food," Lily said. "Poor little loves—they look really lost." Then she laughed as the white kitten let out a loud, squeaky mew. "Was that because I mentioned food? Are you hungry?" She tickled her under the chin, and the white kitten gazed at her in surprise and then mewed again. "Let's get you three into a pen, and then we can try you on a little bit of wet food. They don't look too skinny, do they? Someone must have been taking care of their mom pretty well. I guess they just didn't want the kittens."

The white kitten wriggled and squealed, struggling to get back to her brother and sister. She wanted her mother more, but the other kittens were the only thing that she knew in this strange place. They would have to do.

"Yes, it's okay, here you go." Maria slipped her back into the box with the others. "We'll put the box in the pen with them for the time being, okay? It might help them feel safe."

The white kitten huddled gratefully

with the others, letting them nuzzle her all over. Then the three kittens froze as the box was picked up again. They skidded a little on the cardboard, sinking in their tiny claws and mewing in panic. What was happening? Where were they going now?

"Do you think they're big enough to get out, or should we tip the box on its side?" Maria asked.

"Hmm. Tip it over, I'd say. It will take them a while to climb out, and they might not be able to get back in again. A box isn't much comfort, but it's all they've got at the moment."

Lily reached in and gathered up the kittens in a furry, squeaking mass until Maria had turned the box onto its side, so the kittens could easily step out into their pen. "There! Now you can take a little look around."

The two tabby kittens looked at the open side of the box, and then padded slowly toward it. They peered out and snuffled at the air, then they set off to explore the pen. The white kitten watched them, but she took a while to follow. The box felt safe, and she didn't like the bright lights.

But she didn't like being left alone, either, and at last she stepped out of the box and began to sniff her way around.

She was in the back of the pen, padding her paws on the soft basket, when she smelled food. She hadn't noticed the dish being put into the pen, and she dashed over to join the other kittens. Her tabby sister was actually standing in the food bowl. The white kitten had to eat around her, but she was so hungry that she didn't care.

"Did you see that?" Maria crouched down by the pen to watch the three kittens eating. "She took a long time to notice the food. The other two heard me opening the door, and they rushed right over. The white one just kept looking at the basket."

"Maybe she wasn't as hungry," Lily suggested, but then she shook her head. "No, look at her now, she's eating like she's half-starved."

"Yeah…." Maria snapped her fingers, and the two tabby kittens looked up at once, their ears twitching. It was obvious they'd heard her. When she didn't do anything else, they went back to eating as fast as they could.

The white kitten didn't look up.

"I suppose we should have guessed that she might be deaf," Lily said, looking at the white kitten. "White cats quite often are, and I've heard that if they have blue eyes, it's even more likely. Poor little thing."

"It doesn't seem to bother her,

though," Maria pointed out. "She's just as big as the other two, so it hasn't stopped her from eating."

Lily nodded. "But it's going to make it harder to find her a home."

The white kitten licked around her part of the food dish, and then licked her tabby sister's paws, too. She sat down by the bowl and yawned, showing tiny, needle-sharp teeth.

Then she looked over at the cat bed and stood up slowly. Her stomach looked a lot rounder than it had 10 minutes before, and she rolled a little from side to side as she stomped across the pen. The two tabby kittens gave the empty dish one last lick and then followed her, clambering into the soft cat bed and slumping down together before falling asleep in seconds.

"Maybe it won't be so difficult to find a home for her," Maria said, smiling. "She's so sweet—they all are—but the blue eyes make her even more special. And it isn't all that hard to have an indoor cat. We just need to find the right person." Then she looked thoughtful. "Actually, I might have an idea...."

Chapter Three
A Special Meeting

"Hang on a minute, Abi—that's my phone ringing." Mom put down Abi's homework book and searched under Ruby's pile of drawings for her cell phone.

Abi went back to frowning at her language arts homework and chewing her pencil, but after a moment or two, she looked up and started to listen carefully to Mom's end of the phone call.

36

"Oh, yes, we'd definitely be interested. Yes, I do see that it's harder if she can't go out, and I'll have to talk it over with my husband, but we'd love to take a look."

"I drew a cat!" Ruby announced, holding up her picture to show Abi.

"Nice! Be quiet a minute, Ruby. I want to hear what Mom's saying."

"Yes, I think we could come tomorrow. Is about four thirty okay? I'm a teacher, so I can't usually get back from school before then."

Chris wandered into the kitchen and opened the fridge to get the ingredients for dinner. "Who's your mom talking to?" he whispered to Abi as he pulled out a bag of vegetables.

"I don't know! But we're going

somewhere. And … and it sounds like it might be about a cat…." Abi grabbed his hand and squeezed it tightly, staring at Mom hopefully as she ended the call.

"You guessed who that was, then," she said, looking happily at Abi. "I can tell from your face!"

"Was it the animal rescue?" Abi gasped. "Have they changed their mind? Can we have a cat?"

"Yes! Well, maybe. Chris and I need to talk about it first." She glanced at him. "They have a kitten—an adorable little white one. But she's completely deaf, they think. She'd need to live indoors because she'd never be safe anywhere near a street. So … that was them calling to ask if we'd like to have an indoor kitten."

"An indoor kitten!" Abi breathed. "A white kitten? To be ours?"

"A kitten!" Ruby bounced up and down on her chair and banged a handful of pencils on the table. "A kitten!"

Chris laughed. "At least it wouldn't matter that Ruby's noisy, I suppose. I don't know—how do you keep a cat indoors? I've never even thought about it."

"They said they'd make sure we know everything we'd need to, but we have to understand it's a big commitment," Mom said, looking seriously at Abi and Ruby. "We'd have to be really careful about opening the doors."

"And keeping the windows closed," Abi suggested.

"Yes…." Chris put the pan on the stove and reached for the oil. "We could do that, though, couldn't we?"

"Let's see what they say." Mom glanced at Abi. "Try not to get too excited, sweetheart. It sounds wonderful, but we need to know if we can take care of an indoor kitten before we say yes."

"We can go and see her, though? And find out?" Abi looked hopefully from her mom to Chris and back again, and they nodded. Her mom was smiling.

They might really be able to have a kitten, after all....

Maria led the way along a hallway lined with cat pens. Abi hadn't thought there would be so many. They were almost all full, too. Cats and kittens were lounging in baskets or standing by the wire doors looking back at her.

"Here we are," Maria said, smiling at Abi and Ruby, who was holding Mom's hand and dancing up and down. "This is the white kitten we'd like you to meet."

Abi looked through the door of the pen. There were three kittens in there. Two were tabbies who were rolling around on the floor playing with a toy mouse with a long string tail. The third was a white kitten who was lying in the basket and watching the others. Abi thought she looked very grand compared to the playful tabbies, almost regal.

"She's beautiful," Mom said, sounding a bit surprised.

"Isn't she?" Maria agreed. "And she's very friendly. We've only had them for a couple of days, but she's settled in really well. She loves being petted." She looked at Abi's mom and Chris hopefully. "So if it's okay with you, I'll bring her to one of our meeting rooms, and we can talk about how to take care of a deaf cat."

"That would be great," Chris said. "We'd really like to know more about what we'd need to do. I've been thinking about it ever since you called, and so have the girls. If we can take care of an indoor cat, it wouldn't matter that we live on such a busy street."

"Exactly." Maria nodded. "Another

thing that made us think of you was your registration form. We saw that Chris works from home. Indoor cats need to have someone around for company."

Chris looked pleased. "Yeah, I suppose that makes sense."

Maria nodded. "Okay, if you head to that room at the end there, I'll bring her in."

"Does she have a name?" Abi asked suddenly, looking back from the door of the cat meeting room.

Maria shook her head. "Not yet. They just came in, and we haven't decided on anything yet." She smiled. "So if you adopt her, maybe you could name her."

What would be a good name for a

white cat? Abi wondered as she waited, perched excitedly on the edge of a chair. Snowball and Snowdrop were really cute, but it would be nice to have something a little different. A lot of white cats were named Snowball. She looked around hopefully as the door swung open and Maria came in with the white kitten cuddled in her arms.

"Here we are. Now, like I said, she's very friendly, but she's still little, so be gentle." Maria sat down on the floor with the white kitten standing on her lap. "There you go, little one," she said. "You go and take a look around." Then she smiled at Abi and her family. "I know she can't hear me, but I keep forgetting and I talk to her anyway!"

The white kitten stood there, looking around curiously. *She's so pretty,* Abi thought. Even prettier close up, when you could see how blue her eyes were and the shell-pink of her nose and ears. Even her tiny paws were pinkish.

"So do we have to take care of her differently because she's deaf?" Chris asked.

"Well, you won't be able to call her, and she won't hear food going into her bowl or anything like that. But she can definitely pick up vibrations." Maria slapped her hand on the floor and the kitten looked around curiously. "You see? It's not the noise she's responding to, it's the feel—the vibrations in the air. You can teach her to use hand signals, too, like calling her to come to you, or maybe touching your mouth to say it's time to eat. I've got a handout to give you with some ideas."

"You mean, we can train her?" Abi asked. "Like a dog?" She slipped down off her chair to sit on the floor with Maria, and the white kitten watched her.

"Sure. Cats are really clever. And most cats will do anything for food. If she comes when you call and you give her a treat, she's going to learn that it's a good thing to do."

"Oh, she *is* coming to me," Abi whispered as the white kitten padded across the floor. "Hello, kitten." Then she looked up at Maria. "It seems weird not to talk to her."

"I know what you mean. And of course you still can—just as long as you don't get upset when she doesn't notice. Actually, if you talk, she might understand your body language. Go big on the facial expressions," Maria suggested. "Big smiles if you're pleased with her, and frown if she's jumped up somewhere she shouldn't."

"Is it okay for Abi to pet her?" Mom asked, and Ruby reached toward the kitten. "Me, too!"

"Your turn in a minute, Ruby," Chris said.

"It's fine to pet her—but just tap your fingers on the floor in front of her first, Abi, so you don't startle her. She's looking at you right now anyway, but it's a good idea to get into the habit of showing her you're there."

Abi tapped her nails on the floor, and the kitten put her head to one side, obviously intrigued. She sniffed Abi's fingers and stood still while Abi gently rubbed her little pink ears. Then she began to purr, a huge clickety purr that made Abi laugh.

"She's so noisy!"

"Yes, that's another thing about deaf cats—she can't hear how loud she's being. And it might be that she enjoys the feel of making a noise. She's got a really loud meow, too."

"Ruby, do you want to pet her?" Abi suggested. "She's so soft."

Ruby nodded eagerly and scrambled down from Mom's knee. "Should I tap?" she asked Maria seriously, and Maria smiled at her. "Yes, that would be great. Good job."

The white kitten looked around as Ruby banged the floor and the kitten gazed silently back at her. Abi couldn't believe how good her little sister was being—it was almost as if the kitten had made her shy. Ruby reached out her hand slowly, and the kitten padded forward and licked her fingers.

"Her tongue's all rough!" Ruby whispered. Then she looked at Mom and Chris. "When are we taking her home?"

Chapter Four
Settling In

Abi had hoped they might be able to take the white kitten home right away, once Mom and Chris had signed all the paperwork and paid her adoption fee. But they weren't going to be allowed to have her until the weekend. There was a lot to do first, Chris pointed out as they were driving home. "We need to get her a basket—maybe one of those igloo ones. A litter box, food and water bowls, toys. A scratching post."

"Yes, and we need to walk around the house and think about what we need to do. Maria's going to come back for a visit in a day or two to help us get ready for an indoor kitten," Mom said, turning around to look at Ruby and Abi in the back of the car.

Abi sighed. "Does that mean we have to clean up again?"

Chris snorted with laughter. "Actually, Maria gave me a handout to read about indoor cats while your mom was signing papers. It says that they like a nice cluttered space with a bunch of stuff to hide behind. So our house should be perfect."

"Can I take a look?" Abi asked, and Mom found the handout and passed it back to her. Abi glanced through it. "Wow. There's a lot to learn, isn't there? I didn't know we had to give the kitten grass."

"What?" Chris sounded surprised. "I missed that part. Grass, huh?"

"Yes. It says here that it helps them get the hair out of their stomachs. Why would they have hair in their stomachs, though? Oh, I guess it's because they're always licking themselves. We have to have a little pot of grass for her to nibble on!"

When they got back home, Abi finished reading the handout lying on her bed. There *was* a lot to do. Mom had already said they'd have to get some

sort of screen to put over the windows—
she hated the idea of keeping them all
closed in the summer.

While Mom and Chris were making
dinner, Abi sat at her desk
and started making a
list of everything
they needed
for their
kitten. It
was a long
list, but she
didn't mind.
Every little thing she wrote down
seemed to make the kitten more theirs.
And in a few days' time, they would be
bringing her home.

The white kitten sniffed anxiously at the sides of the box and mewed. She didn't know what was happening, but the last time she had been carried in a box, she had been taken away from her mother. She had been well fed at the rescue, and her brother and sister had been there to snuggle with, but it wasn't the same. With her mother, she had been safe and warm....

The box tipped a little, and the kitten slid into the corner with a frightened squeak. She crouched there, huddled and mewing for what seemed like hours as the box swayed and tipped and lurched. And then it stopped—she was on solid ground again, she could feel it. She sat up and glared as the flaps at the top were opened.

There were faces peering inside, and she crouched back into her corner miserably. She was somewhere new; she could smell it.

"She doesn't look very happy," Abi said. "I wish we'd gotten her one of those special carriers with a wire front so she could see out."

"We will," Mom agreed. "It was just getting a little expensive, buying everything all at once. So when Maria said we could have this box to carry her in, it seemed like a good idea. But you're right, she looks positively upset. Don't you, sweetheart?"

"Get her out," Ruby begged. "I want to cuddle her."

The kitten squeaked again as Mom reached in to lift her out. "I don't think she wants cuddling right now, Ruby. She's a little confused."

"Should we just let her look at her new basket and toys?" Abi suggested. "I thought she'd be happy to have a forever home. But I don't think she understands that's what this is yet."

The kitten slunk across the floor, sniffed cautiously at the igloo basket, and darted inside. Then she crouched down in the opening and peered out suspiciously at the family staring back at her.

Chris sighed but he was grinning, and Abi frowned at him. "What are you smiling like that for?"

"I don't know. I guess I've just never seen a more annoyed-looking cat. She's so tiny and sweet, but every hair on her is annoyed."

"Maybe we should feed her," Mom suggested, and Abi hurried to get one of the new kitten food pouches they'd bought at the store.

The kitten twitched as she saw Abi gently tilting the food bowl toward her. She could smell the food—the same kind that she was used to. She was very hungry…. Slowly, she put her nose out of the basket and eyed the people crowded around. There were too many of them.

"She isn't just upset, she's scared," Abi said suddenly. "We should leave her alone."

"But I want to cuddle her!" Ruby cried.

"Me, too." Abi sighed. "But we have to wait a little while. Look at her, Ruby. She's really frightened. She doesn't even want to come and eat her lunch."

"She's like you were, Ruby, on the first day of preschool," Mom pointed out. "Let's all give her some space."

Ruby sniffed. On her first day of school, she'd had to be bribed with the promise of a new bottle of bubble mixture to stop holding onto Mom's legs, and she still had days where she didn't want to go into the classroom. She tiptoed away from the kitten and

60

sat down on a kitchen chair to watch.

The kitten stepped carefully out of the basket and went to the food bowl. For a little while, she was more interested in the food than she was worried about this strange new place. But once the bowl was empty, she looked around and they were all still there, watching her.

The bigger girl was sitting on the floor with a feather toy in her hand. There had been one of those to play with before. The kittens had loved it, dancing and jumping and falling over each other to catch the feathers and twinkling ribbons.

The shiny ribbons caught the light as the girl shook the toy. The kitten padded closer, just to look. Then the feathers twitched again and she bounced, all four paws off the ground, to catch them. One paw came close, her claws just skimming the edge of the feathers, but the toy jumped away. She crouched down to stalk it across the floor, waiting until the moment was just right. Then she sprang straight up and thumped it hard with her paw.

She landed half in Abi's lap, slipping down her knees. Abi put a hand out to catch her, gently scooping the kitten up.

62

Abi was still holding the stick for the cat toy, and the bundle of feathers was dangling next to her now. The kitten sat up on her hind paws and grabbed it, hugging it tight. She settled back on Abi's lap to chew on the feathers and forgot that she was scared.

"We need to decide what to name her," Chris said, watching Ruby and Abi petting the white kitten, who was stretched out between them on the couch half asleep. They had danced the feather toy around for her all afternoon, and she was worn out. She'd eaten another pouch of kitten food, and she'd figured out where her litter box was. *She's doing great,* Abi thought. Especially since Maria had warned that it might take her days to settle in.

"It should be something to do with her color," Mom suggested. "Or her blue eyes. We could call her Sapphire."

Abi made a face. "That's not very easy to say."

"Sky, then?"

Chris nodded. "That's better."

"My friend Sky would like that," Abi said, tickling the kitten under the chin.

"Oh, I forgot about that…. It might be a little confusing, though. What about Blanche? It's French for white."

Abi wrinkled her nose. "I don't think she looks like a Blanche. She's like—she's like…." Abi sighed. "I don't know! She's so pretty. And I love her pink nose—it's like a flower petal." She looked up at Mom and Chris suddenly. "We could call her Flower!"

Mom looked pleased. "That's a beautiful name."

"Hey, Flower," Abi whispered as she petted the white kitten again. The kitten didn't hear her, of course, but she began to purr, a purr so loud that Abi could feel Flower's whole furry little body shaking under her fingers.

On Sunday, Flower began to explore her way all through the house. It took her a while to get upstairs, as her legs were still a little too short for the steps, but she was determined, and Ruby gave her a lift the last few steps to the top. She sat on Ruby's bed and watched her play and then tried to climb inside the dolls' house. Then she slept on Abi's lap while she did her homework.

Sometimes she sat on the back of the couch and watched the street outside through the front window, but she didn't seem to mind that she was an inside cat. She didn't know any different, Abi decided. Actually, even if they'd adopted a kitten who *wasn't* deaf, it would have had to stay inside for a while, Maria had told them. Kittens couldn't go out until they'd had all their vaccinations.

The handout had been right when it said that indoor cats liked things to hide behind. Flower went under the couch, inside the cupboard where the pans were kept, and almost got stuck behind the bookcase in the living room. She loved climbing, too.

On Monday morning before school, Abi came into the kitchen to get her cereal and looked around to see where Flower was. She'd hurried down before she got dressed and found the kitten still curled up asleep in her igloo basket— but she definitely wasn't there now. It was only when she heard a tiny meow that she realized where Flower was. She was perched on the curtain rod over the kitchen window, and she looked a bit worried.

"Mom!" Abi yelled. "You need to come and see this!"

Flower mewed again and tried to stand up, slipping a little bit.

"How did she get up there?" Mom said, stopping in the doorway to stare.

"I don't know, but I think she's about to fall off! Can you reach her?"

Mom lifted up the kitten and made a frowny face at her, wagging her finger like an angry mother in a cartoon.

"What are you doing?" Abi asked her mom. Then she giggled, watching

Flower stalk across the kitchen floor to her water bowl, pretending she hadn't been stuck at all.

Mom laughed, too. "I was trying to do a big facial expression, like Maria said. So she understood I was not happy with her."

"Ohhh. I'm not sure it was her fault, though. I was reading about deaf cats on the internet, and one of the websites said they liked being high up because it makes them feel safe. Like no one could creep up on them."

"Maybe. But she can't get into the habit of climbing the curtains," Mom said firmly. Then she turned, looking toward the front door. "Oh, no, is that the trash collectors? I haven't put the garbage cans out!" She hurried from the kitchen to open the front door. "Abi, make sure you're holding Flower or watching that she doesn't go out."

Abi crouched down by the kitten, but Flower hadn't even noticed that the front door was open. Abi heard the door close and went to get her cereal. Flower finished her drink and padded out into the hallway.

"I almost missed them!" Mom said, coming back with a relieved look on her face. Then her eyes met Abi's, and they both whirled around at the sound of the front door clicking open.

"It's the garbage truck!" Ruby cried excitedly, waving to the man pulling the trash can away from the front gate. "Hello! Hello!"

The trash collector waved back, and

Ruby jumped up and down happily.
Behind her, a curious white kitten
hurried toward the door, and Abi raced
up the hallway.

"Ruby, don't let her out!"

Ruby turned around, surprised
and then horrified, as
Flower slipped past
her feet. Abi
lunged forward,
grabbing the
white kitten
just before
she shot out
the door.

"Oh, Abi, good
job!" Mom gasped, hurrying down the
hallway after her. "That was close!"

Chapter Five
A Fun Game

"I'd have been so upset with her," Sky said when Abi told her about it later on.

"I was a bit—but Ruby's only little, and she was really upset when Mom explained what she'd done wrong." Abi shook her head. "It's so tricky! I never thought we opened the front door that much. But we do, a lot.

And in the summer we leave the back door to the yard open all the time. Or we did."

Sky made a face. "Are you thinking an indoor cat is going to be too much trouble?"

"No way! We'll just have to be careful. Flower is so beautiful. She's still a little shy sometimes, but we've only had her for a few days. I *think* she likes us."

"Of course she likes you," Sky said encouragingly. "Or she should. It sounds like you're being perfect indoor cat owners."

They were trying, anyway—but it was a lot more work than anyone had expected, even after all they'd done to get ready. After Flower had climbed the curtains for the third time, Mom and Chris decided she needed something of her own to climb. So on Saturday, they went to the pet store to choose a cat tree for her—a special climbing frame for a cat with scratching posts, a box to hide in, and a little hammock to sleep in.

Flower loved it, and the hammock was her new favorite sleeping place, much better than her basket.

She lolled around in it with her paws in the air and her chin hanging over the edge so she could see what was going on.

Abi wasn't sure if Flower was so nosy because of her deafness or if all cats were like that, but the little kitten hated to miss anything. She had to climb and sniff and probably scratch everything that came in the house. She loved Abi and Ruby's room because it was full of toys and blankets and things to explore and snuggle under. Sometimes she slept on Abi's bed, but Mom always came and got her before she and Chris went to bed. Mom wasn't sure that Flower would be able to make it down the stairs when she needed the litter box.

Halfway through Flower's second

week with the family, Ruby brought home a junk model from school. Art was her favorite thing about preschool, but Mom had made a rule—one model in, one model out. Otherwise, Abi and Ruby's room would be completely full of cereal boxes stuck to toilet paper tubes.

The new model was a cat—actually, it was Flower, or so Ruby said. Abi couldn't quite see it, only that there were some soggy pieces of white tissue paper stuck on.

"Flower knows it's her," Ruby said proudly, setting it down on the floor in front of the kitten and watching as she sniffed it and then tried to climb inside the tissue box that was her body.

"You know what?" Abi said

thoughtfully. "There was something like that on one of the websites I was looking at about indoor cats."

Chris looked at her in surprise. "What, making junk models for them to shred? Ruby, if you don't want her to eat it, I'd go and put it somewhere high up in your bedroom."

"Not to claw at. To get food out of." Abi frowned, trying to remember. "It said that outdoor cats spend a long time tracking and hunting, and even if they never actually catch anything, it's good for indoor cats to have something like that, too. That you should make getting their food into a puzzle. There was a picture that looked just like one of Ruby's models. It was all toilet paper rolls stuck together, and there were cat treats hidden inside it. Like the treats Flower sometimes has now."

"That's a great idea." Chris reached out to the back of the kitchen door, where there was a cloth bag hung on a hook. "There you go. We were saving these for Ruby to take to school. *Loads* of toilet paper rolls."

"Can I help?" Ruby asked, cuddling her cardboard cat protectively while Flower pranced around her ankles, purring with excitement.

The pyramid of toilet paper roll tubes was so huge that it took a long time for all the glue to dry. Abi and Ruby had made it very carefully. They cut extra holes in some of the tubes and blocked other ones off halfway with plastic bottle caps so that it was like a kitten intelligence test. When it was finally dry enough to let Flower anywhere near, it became her new favorite toy.

She was asleep in her hammock when Abi gently shook the box of special dry kitten food close by and then tapped her fingers on the box. Flower's eyes snapped open, bright blue against her white fur, and her ears twitched. Even though she couldn't hear, Flower still used her ears for signaling. They twitched *a lot*.

She hopped down the levels of her cat tree and hurried into the kitchen to her food bowl, which was empty. She sniffed at it, confused, and then turned around to stare accusingly at Abi. They had shaken the food box at her—Abi had touched her hand to her mouth, too, the way she always did when there was going to be food. But there wasn't any.

Abi was tapping her fingers on the floor, though, and Flower could still smell cat treats. She sniffed curiously at the pile of cardboard tubes that Abi and Ruby had set down in front of them. That was where the smell was coming from, she was almost sure. She peered in. Yes, there was definitely a cat treat inside, but the tube was just a little too narrow to get her head in. She mewed, and Ruby reached for the treat.

"No, don't get it for her," Abi said. "She needs to figure it out."

With a confused little hiss, Flower stretched up, so she could reach in with one small paw. She scratched around a bit and then hooked the treat, sending it bouncing onto the floor. Then she gobbled it up triumphantly.

"You see!" Abi yelped, high-fiving Ruby. "I told you she'd do it!"

"She's finding more," Ruby said, giggling as Flower almost tipped over the pyramid by standing right up on her hind legs to claw out a treat from the top. "She likes it!"

The cat tree and the food-hunting pyramid were meant to help keep Flower busy inside, so she didn't feel stressed because she couldn't go outdoors. They worked—but not completely. The kitten still loved to sit on the back of the couch and watch the comings and goings in the street. She was fascinated by cars driving up and down outside—Abi could see her following them, turning her head as they sped by.

She still wanted to see what was going on every time someone went to the front door, too. She couldn't *hear* the bell, but

Abi thought she could maybe *feel* it—their doorbell was very loud and sharp. Flower always seemed to come running when it rang, unless she was upstairs.

Abi and Ruby had to pick her up every time the door was answered, or she'd be trying to slip around Mom or Chris's feet. Flower would wriggle eagerly in their arms, her whiskers twitching as she sniffed all those wonderful outdoor smells.

After the incident with the trash collectors, there were a couple of other near-misses where Flower was just so wriggly that Abi couldn't hold on to her. Chris had to shut the door very suddenly on the mail carrier to stop the little kitten from dashing out.

That night at dinner, he told Mom

and Abi and Ruby that he was thinking of building Flower a catio—a cat patio out in the yard with wire sides and a roof so she could sunbathe and explore outdoors.

Abi giggled and looked down at Flower, who was sitting on her lap, hoping Abi would drop pieces of sausage. "I bet she'll still try and get out the front door."

"Of course she will." Chris rolled his eyes. "But it's better than nothing. She obviously really likes the idea of being outside."

A couple of days after her near escape past the mail carrier, Flower was dozing in her hammock, softly flexing her tiny claws in and out as she dreamed. She blinked and squeaked to herself, and half woke up as she felt Chris's heavy footsteps going past the living room, where the cat tree was. She popped her head out, watching him walk into the kitchen, and wondered what he was doing. It didn't *feel* like it was time to eat, but it might be....

She wriggled out of her hammock and hopped down onto the floor, meaning to follow Chris. Then she noticed the shopping bags that he'd left in the hallway. They were just by the living-room door—one big bag full of books and a couple of empty ones. They looked interesting.

She sniffed at them—so many smells!

Food smells and people smells and others she had no idea about.... Flower clawed her way up the side of the largest bag, trying to investigate—and then she realized that she could 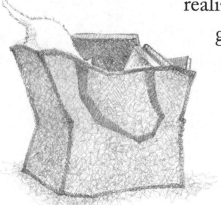 get inside. The bag of books smelled strange, but the plastic stuff they were covered in was good for her claws. She flexed them in and out happily.

Then the footsteps thumped back, and the bags swayed and lifted. There was a rush of cool air.

Flower didn't know it, but she was outside at last.

Chapter Six
Missing!

"Chris—hi!"

The library books shifted under Flower's paws as Chris set the bag down and started chatting to the neighbor who'd waved at him. The bag slumped open, revealing the pile of books and the little white kitten perched between them. Flower peered over the edge of the bag and then hopped out. Chris and the neighbor were too busy talking and complaining about someone dumping an old mattress on the grass down the street to notice her. Flower padded away, sniffing thoughtfully at the cars-and-trucks smell in the air.

She wandered along the pavement, flinching at the rumble of the cars' wheels and the way the air moved as they sped by her. It ruffled her fur and her whiskers, and she knew that they were large and probably dangerous. A big truck went past, scaring her with its heavy rattling vibration, and Flower crouched down by a gatepost, where it felt a little safer.

Then
there was
a sudden
rush of air
and movement
as a car rolled past her
into the driveway, so close
that the ground shook under her paws
and her ears and whiskers were blown
straight back.

The kitten stumbled backward with a
mew of fright. She had never seen a car
so close up—she didn't know what was
happening.

The car's engine was turned off,
and the terrifying shake of the ground
settled to an uneasy nothing. Flower
stayed frozen for a couple of seconds
and then raced away, desperate to

escape the fearful rumbling thing that she was sure had almost flattened her. She dashed wildly along the pavement, shooting around a corner onto a side street and then down a little alley.

The shuddering vibrations of the cars were a little farther away now, and her hammering heart slowed. She flung herself under a clump of scruffy bushes and crouched there among the dead leaves and dust, shivering each time another car shook the ground.

Mom didn't have any meetings after school that day, so she brought Abi and Ruby home, rather than Chris picking them up as he usually did. They opened the front door in the careful, kitten-watching way they'd learned, peering around to make sure that Flower was nowhere nearby, and then hurrying in.

But Flower wasn't anywhere to be found. They searched and searched all over the house, in every cupboard and on top of every bookcase, in all the places they'd ever found her lurking.

"Maybe she's asleep and can't hear us…," Abi said, even though she knew that couldn't be true. Somehow Flower always knew when they were home. She would appear, padding eagerly down the hall and rubbing herself around their ankles until someone picked her up.

"Maybe she got out," Mom said worriedly, looking around as though she expected to see an open window.

"She couldn't have." Chris shook his head. "I checked before I went to the library and the store. She was asleep in her cat tree—and even if she hadn't been, I'd have noticed her sneaking out the door. She has to be here somewhere. She just has to."

But she wasn't, even though they searched everywhere all over again, with Ruby crying and Abi trying very hard not to. At last, even Chris had to admit that Flower wasn't anywhere to be found. "We'd better go and look for her outside," he said, sounding shaken.

"What if she went into the street?"

Abi whispered. She was thinking about what Maria had said—that the road in front of their house was too dangerous for a cat. Any cat, let alone a kitten who couldn't hear and had never been outside before. Not since she was really tiny and been found in a box, anyway.

Mom swallowed. "I'm sure she wouldn't.... She'd be scared. I expect she's hiding in someone's yard. We'll go and look."

They went outside, peering around the front yard, looking under all the bushes and over the fence into the neighbor's yard.

"Flower! Flower!" Ruby called, and Abi glared at her.

"She can't hear you, Ruby! Don't be silly!"

Ruby sniffed loudly and began to cry again. "Abi's being mean to me!"

"You're right, Abi, but you shouldn't shout at Ruby like that," Mom told her. "Actually, I wonder if there *is* a way we can call her. Tapping isn't going to work, not unless she's really close."

"I don't think so. There's too much noise and vibration from the street." Chris shook his head. "And I still don't understand how she could have gotten out. I'm going to walk down the street and look in all the yards. Do you want to come with me, Abi?"

"Yes." Abi nodded. She was so worried and upset that it was making her grumpy, and if she stayed searching their yard, she'd probably snap at Ruby again.

They walked out onto the pavement just as a car raced past, and Abi shivered. She tried to imagine what it would have felt like to Flower if she'd come out onto the pavement—the kitten would have been terrified. Abi leaned over the fence, trying to see around the bushes in the yard next door, while Chris did the same at the house farther down the street.

"Are you all right?"

Abi looked up in surprise. She hadn't noticed their neighbor, Annika, opening her front door. "We've lost our kitten," she explained. "I'm sorry about leaning over your fence—I was looking for her. She's an indoor cat. And she's deaf."

"Oh, no—well, you're welcome to come into the yard and see if you can find her." Annika stepped out onto her front path and crouched down to look around. "What color is she?"

"She's white, and she's really tiny."

Annika looked up, her eyes widening. "A really little white cat? I think I saw her this afternoon!"

"You did?" Abi felt her hands tighten on top of the fence. "Where was she?"

"Running down the sidewalk. She was farther along the street, a few houses down from the supermarket." Annika frowned. "And she was definitely going that way."

Abi stared at her. The supermarket was right at the end of the street. She had been hoping that Flower would be in Annika's yard or possibly the next one over. How could Flower have gone so far? She must have been terrified, with all the cars speeding by on the busy street. "Wh-when was that?" she asked, her voice shaking a little.

"Well, my shift finished at two," Annika said. "So it must have been about half past, I guess." She looked worriedly at Abi. "It might not have been her...," she added gently.

"Did she have blue eyes?" Abi asked, not sure whether to hope Annika would say yes or no.

"I *think* so.... She was running, so I didn't see her for very long...."

"Thanks—I'd better tell Chris." Abi turned to look for her stepdad, but he was already walking back toward them.

"Did Abi explain, Annika? About our cat?" Chris asked.

"Annika saw her!" Abi burst out. "All the way down the street, going toward the supermarket!"

Chris turned around to look, and Abi

saw him make a face without meaning to. He was thinking what she was thinking—that their street joined with another one close by the supermarket, which was even busier. It definitely wasn't somewhere a little deaf kitten wanted to be running around.

"Thanks, Annika. You've been really helpful." Chris nodded to her. "I'm sorry to disturb you. We'll go and look down there for her now."

Abi slipped her hand into his as they walked along, and Chris squeezed her hand. "We'll find her, Abi," he said firmly. "It's going to be okay."

Abi nodded. She wanted to think so, too. But as the cars kept rolling by, she wasn't so sure that her stepdad was right.

Chapter Seven
A Clever Idea

"There must be a better way of looking for her," Chris said, running his fingers through his hair and looking down the street. "This just isn't working."

They'd been out for more than an hour now. Mom and Ruby had helped to start with, but then Ruby got tired and upset and Mom had taken her home for a snack. Abi and Chris had kept on searching. Abi had even dashed back into the house for the tin that they kept the kitten treats in, as she was sure Flower felt the vibrations when they shook them at home. There was probably too much going on for her to notice it out here, but Abi was going to try everything.

"Mom could put a post about Flower on the school parents' online chat," Abi suggested. "The one where people ask about which day is swimming and what to bring for field trips. A lot of people from school live on this street. Someone else might have seen her."

"That's a good idea," Chris agreed. "There are lost cat websites, too—we can add her to those. And if she's still missing tomorrow, we'll make some posters."

"Tomorrow?" Abi heard her voice go high and squeaky. She'd been sure that they would get Flower back that day. They had to. She couldn't imagine her tiny little kitten outside on her own all night.

"We need to go home and have something to eat, Abi," Chris said gently. "It's almost six, and we haven't spoken to anyone else who's seen her. We can come out again after that, but it'll be getting dark soon."

"She'll be easy to see in the dark," Abi said stubbornly, thinking of Flower's pure-white fur.

"I know—it's just so hard when we can't call for her." Chris looked around, frustrated. "She could be right here, waiting for us to find her."

"Don't say that!"

"I'm sorry." He gave Abi a hug. "Come on. Let's go and get some dinner. Mom sent me a text to say it's ready."

"Okay. But I'm coming out to look again afterward."

Chris nodded. "We will."

In the end, Ruby wanted Chris to read her a bedtime story, and she was so miserable about Flower being missing that it was easier not to argue with her. So after Abi nibbled a little bit of pasta, Mom went out with her to look again instead. She got a flashlight from the kitchen drawer because it was just starting to get dark.

They walked down the street,

stopping to tap on gateposts and stamp their feet outside each yard. But no little white shape dashed out to meet them, and Abi's heart seemed to sink a little bit more with every house they passed. It was sitting somewhere on top of her stomach now, and she felt sick with worry.

"I wonder if we should call the animal rescue," Mom said as they reached the supermarket at the end of the street. "Just in case someone found Flower and turned her in."

"But then they'll know we didn't take care of her properly," Abi whispered.

"Oh, Abi, love. I'm sure they won't think that. We've done everything they said...."

"Except we let her out!" Abi gasped. She'd been trying so hard not to cry all this time, but now she couldn't help it. "What if she gets run over? What if she already has been? They said it's happened on this street before...."

"Someone would have seen and told us," Mom said firmly. "And I think the rescue will be closed now anyway. So we can't call them tonight. But I think we'll have to tomorrow morning if we haven't found her by then."

Flower stayed huddled under the bushes. She had peeked out into the darkening alley a few times, but she could still see the blurred lines of cars shooting along the street at the end, and she remembered how one of them had come so close to her. She didn't understand why that had happened, but she dreaded that rumbling rush and the blast of air through her whiskers.

The bushes were
safe, even if her
fur was smeared
with dust. Yes,
she could just
stay here....

But if she
did that, she
wouldn't be able
to get home. Abi and Ruby would
have put food out for her to find,
and she was hungry. She had sniffed
around in the dead leaves for something
to eat, but all she had found was a
beetle that was crunchy and tasted
strange when she'd tried to eat it. She
was so, so hungry. She wanted her food
and to have Ruby dance a toy around
for her, and then be lifted up on Abi's

lap to sleep.

She had to get home. Even if meant going back to that street again.

Abi lay in bed listening to Ruby's snuffled, hiccupy breathing. Ruby had been crying again, and she'd woken up when Abi came to bed and crawled in with her. She'd cried all over Abi's pajamas, so Abi felt damp and even more miserable, and she just couldn't sleep.

"Are you okay, Abi, love?" Mom whispered from the doorway. "Are you awake?"

"A little bit," Abi whispered back.

"We're going to bed now," Mom said,

coming to crouch down by Abi's bed. "Do you want me to put Ruby back in her own bed?"

"No, she'll wake up. It's okay."

"I'm sure we'll find Flower tomorrow." Mom smoothed her hair. "Chris will look for her while we're all at school."

"Okay." Abi didn't know what else to say. She was sure she couldn't spend the day doing reading and math while Flower was still missing. But her mom was a teacher—she was never going to agree to let Abi have the day off from school to keep on looking.

Mom shut the door gently and Abi wriggled a bit, trying to get comfortable next to Ruby. Her little sister snuffled in her sleep and half rolled over so that she was up against the wall. She took most of the comforter with her, and Abi sighed and pulled her old cuddly fleece blanket up around her instead. It smelled comforting, like laundry detergent, and she snuggled it up by her face, sniffing it sadly.

Then she stopped and sat up on her elbow, staring into the darkness.

Smell!

One of the websites she'd read had said deaf cats probably had better other senses than cats who could hear, because they depended on those senses more and practiced using them. And Abi had definitely read somewhere else that one thing you could do for a lost cat was put its bed or litter box outside the house, because cats had incredible noses and would smell their own scent and find their way home.

So Flower would be even better at that than an ordinary cat, wouldn't she?

Abi slid carefully out of bed, trying not to wake Ruby, and wrapped her blanket around her shoulders. She hesitated on the landing outside Mom and Chris's room—should she wake them up? If she did, they'd probably go and put the litter box outside and tell her to go back to bed.

But Abi wanted to be there—she wanted to watch, in case it worked. What if they put the litter box outside and went back to bed, and then Flower came? She wouldn't understand why her litter box was there and nobody was waiting for her. She might go away again.

So Abi tiptoed down the stairs and into the kitchen to grab the litter box. Luckily, no one had cleaned it out—it didn't smell like much to Abi, but she bet Flower would be able to smell it for

miles. She hoped so, anyway. This had
to work. It just had to.

She unlocked the front door carefully
and couldn't stop herself from glancing
around to make sure Flower wasn't
racing down the hallway to see what
was happening. "Silly,"
she muttered to herself.
Then she slipped outside,
shivering in the night air,
and set the box
down on the
path.

She stood
on the path,
looking up and down the
street, hoping to see a little
white shape hurrying
toward her through the darkness, but

there was no one around. It was eerie.

Abi retreated indoors so she could watch from the living-room window. She sat down on the couch right next to where Flower liked to sit. Her eyes were adjusting to the darkness now, and she was sure she could see a few of Flower's white hairs against the dark fabric. She kneeled on the cushions, leaning her elbows on the back of the couch, and stared determinedly out the window.

She was going to stay awake until Flower came home.

Chapter Eight
Home Again

Flower stepped out from underneath the bushes and looked down the alley. It was completely dark now, and she'd been getting colder and colder huddled there. She felt stiff, and slow, and she wasn't sure she could run away if one of those rumbling things came near her again. But to get back home, she supposed she would have to go along the street and risk it. She padded down the dark alley and then flinched as something ran in front of her. She had a moment's glimpse of white teeth gleaming, and a huge paw swept the air in front of her nose, cuffing her and knocking her sideways. She jumped and twisted and rolled over, landing half on her side as the creature loomed over her. Then it darted away.

Flower lay crouched and gasping in the dust, making herself as small as she could, wondering if the creature was going to come back. What was it? Another cat? It must have been. The smell seemed right, but it had been so much larger than she was. She wasn't sure if she should stay still, or run, or try to hide. But the cat seemed to have moved on, and even though there were scents of other animals around, there was nothing else nearby.

At last she began to move forward again, creeping cautiously along the alley to the road. And then she stopped, almost forgetting how much the larger cat had scared her. She had expected the street to be busy and scary. She had been steeling herself for the speed of the cars and the way they made the air whoosh past her whiskers.

She hadn't expected to be lost.

Which way should she turn out of the alley? Which way was home? Which way back to Abi and Ruby? Flower felt the fur rising along her spine again and her tail fluffing up in panic. She was lost, and there were more cats around—she could smell them. She was in their territory. Her territory was the house, and her basket, and the cat tree, and Abi. She was in the wrong place.

Flower hurried out of the alley and stood on the pavement, sniffing anxiously for the other cats' scent. She needed to get out of here. She had been lucky to be left alone all that time she was hidden under the bushes. But which way should she go now?

Her ears flattened against her skull as she realized that she needed to go toward the rumbling, shaking street, the busier street that she had run down. Home was that way, no matter how much she hated the thought of it.

Whiskers bristling, she scurried

down the street, darting along the innermost edge of the pavement in the shadow of the walls along each yard. When she came to the corner, she peered cautiously around at the cars speeding along the bigger street. Then she pressed herself against the wall with a mew of fright as a car turned into the side street toward her. But it rumbled on past without coming any closer.

Which way? Flower huddled against the wall, trying to stay calm and ignore the instinct inside that told her to just run and run, to get away from the cars. But that wasn't going to get her back to Abi and Ruby. After a few moments, she grew a little more used to the cars, and her fur began to lay flat again. She turned her head, trying to smell the way back home.

There was *something*.... Flower grimaced, opening her mouth and curling her muzzle back over her teeth to smell better. She could smell *herself*. Her home—her territory. She bolted along the pavement, following the scent blowing on the wind. She was getting closer—the smell was stronger, and she could feel it—she was almost home.

At last—there it was! Her litter box.
But outside the house, not where it
was meant to be. Flower padded into
the front yard, sniffing at the litter box
cautiously. What was it doing out here?
And how was she going to get into the
house? She went over to sniff at the
door—this was the way she had come
out, carried in that bag. But now it was
closed, and it didn't move even when
she scratched at it and mewed.

Flower sat down on the
doorstep, feeling cold
and even hungrier now
that she was so close
to her food bowl.
She mewed again,
even louder, but still
no one came.

Was there another way she could get in? Wearily, she turned and walked back down the path, looking at the big pot of flowers by the front door and the window up above. She knew that window—it was where she sat to watch the street and the people passing by. Except now she was on the other side, looking in....

She sprang up onto the edge of the flowerpot and made a clumsy jump onto the windowsill. Then she peered through the glass. There was the couch.... Flower mewed loudly in frustration and then pressed her nose closer toward the glass.

Abi was there! She was asleep, her head pillowed on the back of the couch, on the other side of the glass.

Flower stood up on her back paws, mewing and mewing, batting at the glass with her front ones. She could *see* Abi—so why wouldn't Abi wake up and notice her?

Abi was dreaming that she was running down the street after her little white kitten, always just too far away to catch her before she disappeared. She was calling and calling, but all the time, she knew it was useless—Flower couldn't hear her. It was heartbreaking. Flower was so frightened. Abi could hear her mewing in the dream, and the noise was frantic. Flower was racing so fast that her paws were thudding on the ground....

Abi blinked and sat up a little, dazed with sleep. She had been dreaming that Flower was lost. No.... She swallowed miserably. That wasn't a dream—her kitten really *was* lost.

She looked around, confused about where she was—and then she remembered. The litter box outside. She had been trying to give Flower a scent to follow.... Abi shook her head, trying to wake herself up. She hadn't meant to go to sleep, and she could still hear the mewing from her dream. It was even getting louder, and she could hear the thumping paws, too....

"Flower?" Abi stared. Her kitten was there on the other side of the window, paws scratching eagerly, her mouth wide open in a mew.

Abi jumped off the couch, trailing her blanket, and raced for the front door, fumbling with the locks. At last she pulled it open and Flower darted in, purring. She stood up, patting at Abi's knees with her little white paws until Abi picked her up and snuggled them both in the blanket.

Abi blinked as the upstairs light went on, and the glow spread down the stairs.

"Mommy!" Ruby called from the top of the staircase. "Dad! Abi found Flower!" She stumbled down to hug Abi and rub Flower's nose.

"She came back," Abi told her little sister. "She's so clever—she followed her own smell. Oh, she must be hungry." She tapped her mouth—the food sign they always used to show Flower it was time for a meal—and the white kitten stared back at her seriously. Then she lifted her paw and tapped it against her own mouth.

"She did the sign!" Ruby gasped.

"She couldn't have…." Abi looked at

Flower and tapped her mouth again.

The kitten patted her own mouth with her paw and then wriggled out of Abi's arms. She jumped to the floor and dashed into the kitchen to stand by her food bowl.

Abi grabbed one of the pouches from the cupboard and emptied it into the bowl, and the two girls crouched by the food to watch Flower eat. Abi could hear Mom and Chris coming downstairs, and then Ruby dash out to tell them about Flower signing back.

"I'm so glad you found your way home," she whispered to Flower as the kitten licked the last bits of food from around the edges of her bowl. "You're so clever. But please don't ever do that again. And we'll be more careful, too."

Flower padded toward her and climbed up into Abi's lap, licking lazily at one paw and sweeping it around her whiskers. Then she looked up at Abi with her huge blue eyes and began to purr.